JOHN BERGER

Lilac and Flag

An Old Wives' Tale of a City

PART THREE OF A TRILOGY

GRANTA BOOKS
LONDON
in association with
PENGUIN BOOKS

GRANTA BOOKS
2/3 Hanover Yard, Noel Road, Islington, London N1 8BE

Published in association with the Penguin Group
Penguin Books Ltd, 27 Wrights Lane, London W8 5TZ, England
Viking Penguin, a division of Penguin Books USA Inc.,
375 Hudson Street, New York 10014, USA
Penguin Books Australia Ltd, Ringwood, Victoria, Australia
Penguin Books Canada Ltd, 2801 John Street, Markham,
Ontario, Canada L3R 1B4
Penguin Books (NZ) Ltd, 182–190 Wairau Road,
Auckland 10, New Zealand

Penguin Books Ltd, Registered Offices: Harmondsworth, Middlesex,
England

Originally published in the USA by Pantheon Books,
a division of Random House, Inc. 1990
First published in Great Britain by Granta Books 1990
This edition published 1992
1 3 5 7 9 10 8 6 4 2

Printed in England by Clays Ltd, St Ives plc

acknowledgements

Lilac and Flag is the last book of the trilogy *Into Their Labours*, which has occupied me during the last fifteen years. During this long period, Tom Engelhardt has edited my books. Dear Tom, you have encouraged, corrected, and upheld me. Thank you.

Perhaps I would never have had the courage to begin the project if I had not received, before a page was written and until today, the support of the Transnational Institute in Amsterdam. To everyone in Paulus Potterstraat and Connecticut Avenue and to Saul Landau, thank you.

old love poem

The hay
smelt of how
the sky loved the earth.
You were the pain in my ribs
aching
from the carts unloaded.

The dead
were filling a doorway
with the view beyond.
You were the house
the candle under the plum tree
and my eternity.

for Katya and Orestes

birth

Three butterflies rise from the field like white ash above a fire. Let my dead help me now. One of them reappears and, flying over the tall grass which I will soon have to scythe, alights on a blue flower and opens its wings. On each of her wings the same sign is printed in blackish grey—the grey of the first marks if you draw with a burnt stick on paper. I begin to think of Zsuzsa—or perhaps it is she who begins to think of me. A second butterfly comes down and covers the first; the second one is Sucus. The two of them, wings spread, quiver like four pages of a book open in the wind. Suddenly Sucus flies off. Let my dead help me now. Zsuzsa shuts her wings, slips off the scabious flower, and joins the other two butterflies to fly away over the tall grass which I will soon have to scythe. I have loved them all.

food

Zsuzsa lived in a house on the hill behind the tanneries. They were tall, open buildings without walls and on each floor the hides were hung to dry in the salt wind that came off the sea. The hides, bulging a little in the wind, looked like giant bats suspended upside down and asleep. For years there had been talk of pulling down the old tanneries and building new ones elsewhere, further away from the coast. The plan had not been carried out because of a warning from the city health department. If the old sheds were destroyed, so the health department threatened, the million rats who lived and bred there would quit the hill and invade Troy. It was in these tanneries that Marius worked long ago, when many men still came back alive from the city.

On Rat Hill, Zsuzsa's mother's house was blue. Uncle Dima, who sometimes worked in the docks, had painted it with stolen paint, manufactured specially for swimming pools. A bright turquoise blue.

All we need now is the diving board! said Zsuzsa after he had finished painting the house.

A week later Uncle Dima was arrested when he and two of his friends tried to break the till of an all-night garage on the Trojan ring road.

Zsuzsa's father had disappeared five years earlier, without a trace. On the roads between cities people often vanish. Here in the village men leave their wives and their children, but in the end there's always news of them. Two years after Zsuzsa's father had vanished without a trace, her mother came home one Sunday morning with Uncle Dima. Meet my fresh hide, she announced to her son, Naisi, and her two daughters.

The Blue House had two rooms. Compared to some of the neighbours' shacks, it was a solid home. Its walls were made of concrete blocks, and its roof of tarpaulin, stolen from the American navy, was well tarred and held down by wooden batons.

Unlike her younger sister, Zsuzsa was skinny. Not just her wrists and ankles, but her shoulders, her chest, and hips.

She could slip between a door and its hinges, her mother complained.

People say bodies reveal character. They are wrong. Bodies are dealt out to us like cards. Character begins with how you play what you get. At nineteen Zsuzsa looked like a boy. Yet she was already more feminine than any wet nurse. This is what made her a law unto herself.

The first time she met Sucus was outside St. Joseph's. St. Joseph's was not a church but a prison, a large one which held two thousand prisoners. She had been to visit the uncle.

How do you feel, Uncle Dima?

How in God's name do you think?

Bad?

Couldn't be worse.

It's sunny today.

Eleven fucking months. What have you brought me?

Meat pies, a pineapple, smoked cod's liver.

Cod's liver! God in heaven! Who but your mother would think of smoked cod's liver?

Here are some cigarettes.

Zsuzsa, I want you to go and see Rico.

I hate that man, Uncle Dima.

Hate my friend?

Last time he tried to lay me.

Keep out of his reach, that's all. I want you to go and see Rico and I want you to tell him: The truck's ready.

Okay.

What'll you tell him?

He can fetch the truck.

No! The truck's ready.

Same thing.

Dear God, what did your mother do to deserve such an idiot of a daughter. The truck's ready.

I'll tell him, Uncle. Don't worry. Someone has to fetch it, no?

Just tell him: The truck's ready. He'll understand.

I must be off.

Give me a kiss.

It's not allowed here.

Give me your hand then.

Bye, Uncle.

Bye, Zsuzsa. Don't forget.

The gatehouse to the prison, which was a hundred years old, was built in brick. Over the arch above the massive doors, which only opened for black vans bringing in and taking out prisoners, was a wooden panel on which the sign-writer had written STATE PENITENTIARY CORRECTIONAL CENTRE. Above these noble letters he had painted a pair of scales in gold. People on foot entered and left by a small door set, like a reprieve, within one of the large ones. Prison suppliers and undertakers used an electronic entrance to the modern wing, which was at another level, lower down the hill.

From the Champ-de-Mars, outside the main gate, you could see the docks, the district around the railway station known as Budapest, and the industrial area to the north, over which, during the dog days of summer when the sea was like a lake, there often hung a pall of yellowish smoke the colour of smoked haddock. On leaving the prison Zsuzsa came through the little door which was like a reprieve. Outside stood two soldiers.

Their heads turned with their eyes as Zsuzsa walked past. She was dressed in sandals, blue jeans, and a T-shirt with the words STANFORD UNIVERSITY written across it. They quizzed each letter of the unpronounceable words. The fingers of one drummed on the barrel of a submachine gun held in the crook of his arm.

Nice pair of lemons there!

I am an old woman, yet I still remember what it was like to pass by the gaze of men who wanted you—hatefully or beautifully. We give birth to monsters, to saints, and to everybody else who is neither one nor the other. To Jesus of Nazareth and to Herod. Every kind of good and evil comes out from between our legs, and when we are young, every kind of good and evil dreams of getting in there again.

The soldier knew Zsuzsa heard what he said by the change in the way she walked. Further off, some children were playing with a donkey. In the heavy heat the national flag hung limply from its flagstaff on the prison tower.

A nice pair of little lemons!

The second soldier followed Zsuzsa. Suddenly there appeared, as if he had come from heaven to save her, a young man, standing by a low wall on which was placed a painted tray with glasses and a blue thermos.

Would you like a coffee?

How much?

Six hundred.

No.

Better a little lemon juice! said the soldier, leering.

The young man with the painted tray handed Zsuzsa a glass of coffee, and placed himself firmly between the soldier and her.

Drink it, he said. I'm making you a present.

What's your name?

Sucus.

That's a funny name for a boy!

They gave it to me when I was a kid because I sold sweets.

Sucus—a kind of sweet?

You've got it.

The soldier banged the butt of his gun with the palm of his hand and turned his back on them.

Now you sell coffee.

I pay five thousand for this plank.

Who to?

Sucus nodded towards the guards.

It's a lot of money.

Men are willing to pay for coffee here.

Yes?

On their way out, not on their way in. A man who's done his time in there needs a coffee when he comes out to make sure he's not dreaming. He needs a coffee almost as badly as he needs a woman. Then there are the visitors—they need a coffee to prove to themselves they're not like the man they've been talking to. Your one inside—who's he?

My lover man, she lied.

How long's he in for?

Ten years.

He'll go mad.

A flock of starlings—like a thousand black chips of wood flying up from the blow of an axe—crossed the Champ-de-Mars and settled on the black tile rooves of the prison.

They don't, said Zsuzsa. That's the first thing that changes the other side of those gates. Your need to go mad slowly disappears, day by day it gets smaller and smaller, less pressing—she put the palms of her hands against her temples, she wore four rings and her nails were silver-varnished—until one day it goes away. It's outside people go mad. More likely it's me who'll go mad first.

What's his name?

She hesitated, glanced around, and following the flight of the last starlings, saw the national flag hanging limply from the prison tower in the afternoon heat.

Flag, she said.

Flag's his name?

He's called Flag, I tell you.

Strange name.

It came from how he was born. He was born in the street, on June 7th, the national holiday. There were flags everywhere, and he came a month before he was due, a whole month. It was evening and his mother was dancing in Alexanderplatz like everyone else that night . . .

Who told you this?

Suddenly there was lightning and a rumble of thunder over the hills! And her waters broke.

Sucus looked at her face. She had large eyes, too large. She closed them. He knew they were dark, but he couldn't remember their colour. Were they grey or brown?

And there, before you could say Jack Knife, under a roller coaster, behind a rifle range where you could win a life-size doll or a bear cub if you were a good shot, she gave birth on the grass! They were firing all the time, she told me, and the problem was there was nothing to wrap him in, so they took a flag from a street lamp and wrapped him in that. And ever afterwards this was his name, he's called Flag.

Why's he inside, this Flag of yours?

He killed a man.

Deliberately?

Only women kill men deliberately.

Are you sure?

I'm sure.

What did he do, this Flag?

The man was stabbed. Flag was jealous.

Because of you?

Zsuzsa closed her eyes again. Then she said, Yes, because of me.

And the man? Not Flag, the other one.

The other one never touched me. I never let him.

So this Flag was jealous for nothing.

Flag burnt with jealousy for me.

And the other man died?

Yes.

Zsuzsa had two lower teeth missing, he could see this when she smiled.

I don't believe you.

The coffee was very good, said Zsuzsa.

I don't believe you.

Yes, really, it was good, the best I've drunk for a week.

I don't believe your story about Flag.

I'm not asking you to believe anything, she said.

More likely you went to visit little brother who got nicked for car radios. Where do you live, anyway?

Barbek.

On the hill?

Rat Hill.

I live across the river, he said, in Cachan.

Cachan—Zsuzsa exclaimed. That's where my mother works every night.

There's no end to Cachan.

She's a cleaner. In the I.B.M. building. Her last job before daybreak is to change the roses in the sales director's office. He has new roses every day, and the old ones she brings home. Roses I adore. You can give me a hundred. A hundred stolen roses and I'm yours.

Look, said Sucus, nodding towards the prison, there's a man coming out.

The man was carrying a suitcase.

Watch now, the guards'll needle him.

The man held his free arm a little away from his body as if he were walking on a narrow plank high above the ground and had to balance himself. His neck was stiff and he looked straight ahead.

There he goes! said one of the soldiers. The fucker thinks they'll still remember him at home.

The man continued walking, little step by little step, as if along a plank from a boat to the quayside.

Fuckers like him don't deserve a home!

His mother's cunt smells of codfish, said the second soldier.

The man was now through the gate. He could see the whole Champ-de-Mars, the plane trees, the city of Troy below, the children playing with the donkey, Sucus with his painted tray, and the wine-dark sea. He was still walking as if along the plank.

You don't know what his mother's cunt smells of?

A glass of coffee, milord? proposed Zsuzsa.

The freed prisoner hesitated and pulled a handkerchief out of his pocket.

The first taste of freedom, Zsuzsa said.

Black without sugar, said the man.

He held the glass in both hands with the handkerchief wrapped round it, and sat on the low wall to drink slowly, savouring the coffee.

No arsenic in it?

Zsuzsa laughed and Sucus thought: When she laughs, we're taller than anybody.

You haven't heard? said the man. The chief of police was

hospitalised last week. Arsenic poisoning. His wife confessed. There were four women in it together. They had the idea of putting arsenic in their husbands' coffee. A small dose each day. All the husbands were in the law. Bogeys.

They wanted to kill them?

Not at all. They wanted to do a bad turn to Old King Cole.

Who's he?

They wanted to put an end—this is how they said it—to their husbands' infidelities. They'd heard that a little arsenic makes Old King Cole go limp. This way their men wouldn't screw other women. One of the wives put arsenic in her husband's custard too. You need sugar to hide the bad taste of arsenic. That's why I don't take sugar.

Zsuzsa laughed and Sucus thought again: When she laughs, we're taller than anybody.

At first you're frightened, the man said.

Now? she asked.

Of not knowing which way to go.

He opened his battered suitcase and took out a packet wrapped in newspaper.

You lose the habit of choosing, he said.

Inside the newspaper was a leather cap, new-looking and very flat, which he placed painstakingly on the very top of his head, feeling the sides of his shaved scalp with his blunt fingertips so as to measure how high up the cap was.

Zsuzsa handed him a mirror from her handbag. The freed prisoner looked into it and saw a man in his sixties with wild eyes.

It suits you, she said.

You think so? I don't want to turn a corner and run slap into my old crap.

If you're wearing that, no crap will recognise you, she said.

A cap against the crap! the man joked. His eyes were wild with loss.

Everything's good today.

How much do I owe you for the coffee?

Twelve hundred, Zsuzsa said.

The man paid her, shut the suitcase, touched with his fingertips the cap on his head and walked down towards the city.

I didn't believe it, said Sucus. I didn't believe it when you charged him double.

Inside they hear about prices going up, said Zsuzsa, but they lose count of what things really cost outside. They're like babies when they come out.

. . .

Thousands of people were strolling after work beneath the massive trees, through which the streetlamps looked like moons. The shop windows, whose lights only went out at dawn, displayed silver shoes, leather boots, raincoats, handbags, necklaces, document cases, bottles of perfume, cars with convertible rooves, hair dryers, bridal suites, candelabra, VCRs, and real orange trees. Above the shop windows towered buildings with glass walls as high as glaciers. Through them you could see the floors of the offices, neither in darkness nor illuminated but filled with a diffuse grey light, like a television screen has when it's switched on without a picture.

Do you know who goes to the café over there? asked Zsuzsa.

Who?

Coglioni.

Him. He could buy up the whole café.

He doesn't pay a sou. They never charge him.

Like that they keep out of trouble, said Sucus. Let's sit down and order something. When they bring the bill, we'll say we're friends of Coglioni.

His children, we're his children! said Zsuzsa.

He had so many nobody can count them.

How old are you? asked Zsuzsa.

Same age as your Flag.

He led her to an empty table and pulled back a chair for her, as men in white suits do on television.

Whiskey for me; what about you?

I'll have an ice cream—one of those large ones with different colours like a hat.

With a long silver spoon?

With a long silver spoon, she repeated, putting out her tongue at him.

At the next table sat two women, wearing white lace gloves. They stared at the couple who had just arrived.

Nowhere's left, one of them whispered, her lipstick was as red as the handle of a hammer, there's nowhere left these days where one feels safe.

What alarmed the two ladies was the fact that the man with his studded belt and the young woman, who had been walking barefoot, were too close. Far too close. They should have been in another part of the city, not at the next table.

Supposing we order something to eat at the same time? Zsuzsa suggested.

Risky, replied Sucus.

Would you like her portrait done?

All Sucus saw when he first looked up were two thin, hairy legs, then a pair of shorts, skimpy as a loin cloth, and finally a long, bearded face.

No, said Sucus, we don't like portraits.

It'll only take a few minutes.

The man was already pulling a chair towards the table.

You're wasting your time.

Your friend has a face that cries out to be drawn. Behind his beard the man had bulbous lips that were almost blue.

Look, mister, I don't know who you are, but I'll tell you something: we can pull faster ones than you. Leave us alone. Get!

The man sat down and laid his portfolio on the table.

I want to draw your friend because she's so beautiful.

This one isn't for drawing.

I'll make you a present of it when it's done.

Like hell you will.

I won't charge for the drawing. Just give me ten minutes.

How much do you charge usually?

It depends.

You're talking to a systems man. How much do you charge?

Twenty-five thousand.

That's class. Did you hear him, sweetheart? He can sell your mug for twenty-five ribs. Supposing you unbutton a bit? Give them their money's worth for fifty ribs.

The man took a drawing pad out of his folio and opened an old cigarette tin.

What's your name, three-letter man?

Raphaele. And yours?

Flag!

When Sucus said this, Zsuzsa wanted to jump in the air. Instead, she bit on one of her four rings and lowered her eyes.

The man took a pencil out of the tin and began to draw.

Not so fast, Mr. Raphaele! Nothing to stop you doing a second one as soon as we've gone. If you press hard enough with your pencil, you can trace it out again on the page underneath. I wasn't born yesterday. You can make a hundred drawings out of one, and at twenty-five ribs each, that's two and a half million!

Do you know why I'm drawing your friend?

You want to get a hard-on and make money out of it as well?

She has an extraordinary face.

A model has to be paid, just like everyone else, said Sucus.

Let him draw me, Flag.

After a while the waiter came. He suffered from varicose veins and had eyes that were tired of sorting out chits, glasses, coins, people. He noticed Sucus's hands, Zsuzsa's feet, the draughtsman's wrist watch, his expensive Italian sandals. Because of the last two items, he would serve them.

A coffee, said Raphaele.

A whiskey, said Sucus, and an Arctic Glory.

Take no notice of me, said Raphaele to Zsuzsa, carry on as if I wasn't here.

It's not the same as a photo, she said.

Don't look at me, look at Flag.

She looked at Sucus. He was built like a peasant, with sturdy legs and a way of holding his head so that there was space on either shoulder for carrying a sack. She wondered how long he had worn a moustache.

The waiter came back with their orders on a tray.

If I eat my ice you won't be able to draw me, Zsuzsa said, the spoon already in her mouth.

The waiter handed the bill to the bearded man with the Italian sandals. The man paid without saying a word. Sucus winked at Zsuzsa and squeezed her knee.

Now, I don't have to give you the drawing, said the man.

You only paid five thousand, said Sucus. She gives ten minutes for that, no more! You've already had nine. So scribble quick, mister, or order us another round.

Keep the spoon in your mouth a moment!

She studied Flag again. Nobody would ever be able to lay their hands on him, she thought. All his features were as alert as a dog's ears.

The man held up the finished drawing.

I don't look like that! screamed Zsuzsa.

You've made her look like a whore! said Sucus.

You don't like it?

I wouldn't wipe my arse on it.

So there's no point in giving it to you?

You owe her eight thousand for sitting there for you.

That's impossible, twinkie.

You're going to pay, man, either in money or in pain.

Sucus slipped a knife out of his pocket and slid it under his hand onto the table so the man could see it.

Kill me. I love you, said the tall man in shorts.

The grey cat is sitting on my lap, asleep. He's a strange colour. I've never seen another like him. He looks as if he's wearing threadbare greyish underwear through which you glimpse a pale white skin that's never seen the sun. In fact, he has plenty of fur. Indeed, he has two furs, one grey and one white. But instead of the two colours making a pattern, with white patches here and grey patches there, they've grown together like clover and grass. He was born this way. Something wasn't decided properly.

It was then that Zsuzsa noticed the waiter. He was hurrying towards their table with a bogey in plain clothes.

Let's run, she whispered, and snatching the drawing, she pulled Sucus towards a row of little trees in painted white tubs at the edge of the terrace. From there she hopped like a magpie to the pavement below and waited for him.

They left the big avenues and took small roads that went steeply down through the Escorial. In the district of the Escorial there were trees everywhere: magnolias, viburnums, New Red cherries, forsythia, Persian lilacs, maples. Between the flowering branches were lawns, greener in the summer than anything else in Troy because they were watered for hours on end every day. The lawns surrounded swimming pools, painted the same blue as the walls of Zsuzsa's house. Around the pools people gathered before dinner to drink aperitifs. After dinner, when they had drunk some more, they often dove into the water naked. The water was often lit up from underneath so that the pools glowed like precious stones. Many a marriage in Escorial was decided naked in a swimming pool at night.

I'll explain to you how I see things, said Sucus, and your life will never be the same again. Everyone needs something, yes? Everyone needs some little thing to make them a bit happier or a bit less sad. They don't talk about it. Usually they can't get it themselves. To discover somebody's real need, even a little one, requires talent.

I know what you've got tattooed on your biceps—three testicles!

Okay. Listen. When you've discovered the little needs of twenty people, and when you know where to go to fetch them satisfaction, then you've got a living. Because however poor they are, they pay. If not in money, then in something. They come to depend on you. You've got to keep it secret, absolutely secret. If you start talking, another supplier will be there one day before you. And besides, people are ashamed of their needs.

And what do you supply?

Anything. Listen, out in Chicago the water's turned off every night, right? Most people leave for work before it's turned on. A friend of mine goes round to a hundred flats at midday flushing toilets full of morning shit. And in each flat they've left something for him on the kitchen table.

He could snitch whatever he wanted.

No, he couldn't. One, he's blind. And two, everyone knows where to find him. He lives on the estate.

What do you supply? Besides coffee.

I'm looking. Everyone needs something.

Everyone needs everything, Flag.

From behind a hedge of rhododendra they heard laughing. Along the edge of the road, beside each metal gate, the electronic bell and digital control panels were already lit up like spaceship candles.

You see those roses? asked Sucus.

They're Snow Queens.

I'll lift you up.

Ouch! You're hurting.

I'll kneel, said Sucus.

Give me a hand for my foot.

Hold on to my head.

She sat on his shoulders and he straightened his back. Then he held on to her heels, which were as warm as sand the sun had shone on all day.

Watch the thorns!

I've got two!

With the roses pinned to her T-shirt, they walked farther down the hill towards the sea. It was well and truly night. From the air Troy would have looked like jewelry laid out on black velvet.

When did you last eat? he asked.

You mean the Arctic Glory!

A meal, not an ice cream!

I got up late this morning. There was no special reason for getting up. I thought of washing my hair, then I remembered Mother had used the last of the shampoo. I had to visit Uncle but visits to that place are at four o'clock exact. I didn't get out of bed till midday. When I got up I made myself a croque monsieur.

She was holding his hand as they walked and she brought it to her mouth with her two missing teeth and pretended to bite it.

A croque monsieur, she said laughing. And you?

Yesterday.

You must be starving!

I'll tell you what I'd like to eat, said Sucus. I'd like to eat a plate of calamari to start with. Calamari, fried in fresh oil with parsley. Then I'll take a steak because I haven't seen a steak since Easter. No, I'll tell you what I really like. It's goose. I only ate it once in my life—at a wedding.

One day I'll make you my dish of brown beans, said Zsuzsa, I learnt it from my grandmother. I cook the beans all night very slowly, very slowly. And when they're cool in the morning I add crushed garlic and lemon juice and salt them and oil them and I pepper them and I give them to you with hard-boiled eggs which I've cooked all night too, with onion skins and with oil on the water so it doesn't turn into steam.

What's it called this night dish of yours?

Flag's ful medames.

They were at the bottom of the Escorial hill, at the point where the army barracks hid the sea from the road.

How much crash have you got?

Two thousand, and you?

Your coffee money, she said, that's all.

Under the next street light several cars were parked. Sucus tried their doors; they were all locked. It was then, as they went on walking, that an idea came to Zsuzsa. If they continued for a mile, they'd reach the docks. She knew the café where Rico hung out. She had been there a few times with her uncle. She'd deliver the message. Fetch the truck. No. The truck's ready. If Rico, the man with ears like empty saddlebags, started in on his usual tricks, she knew how to get round him tonight. She'd make happen what she wanted to happen. Tonight she wanted to make food for Flag.

No! she said out loud.

She didn't want to make food for Flag, what she wanted was to be food for Flag. She wanted calamari and oil and parsley to come out of her body. She might get a goose out of it too. A goose like her grandmother's. A bird who gave white feathers for a pillow and brown flesh when cooked. She'd give Flag the tenderest morsel, the breast—where he was fingering her now through her T-shirt.

The road followed the railway lines that went to the Customs House, a building as large as twenty barns. On the other side of a wire grill were parked several jeeps with soldiers in them.

Give me an hour? said Zsuzsa.

What do you mean?

I have to go to a café over there. You wait here, and I'll be back in an hour.

I can't see any café. I'll come with you.

It wouldn't work with you.

Then do it tomorrow.

I want to do it now.

And I wait here like a post?

Lie on the grass. She nodded at a waste lot on the other side of the road. I'll be back in an hour.

If you're not, you won't find me.

I promise. Here, keep the drawing for me. I'm going to give it to my children. And let me tell you something you don't know yet, Flag. If Zsuzsa makes a promise, you can depend on it.

She walked away towards the quayside which started after the customs compound. Sucus crossed the road and clambered up a bank. From the top he could see distant white arc lights where they were loading a ship. It was very quiet. He could hear the soldiers across the road talking. He lay down on the grass and looked up at the stars.

In the sky he saw a boat. The varnished white wood of her deck glowed, the colour of resin and honey, and the boards fitted so tightly together, there was only a hairline between them. The ship's deck was the flat stomach of the woman he'd met outside St. Joseph's and the bowsprit was her crossed ankles.

If you are asking how an old woman like me can know what Sucus dreamt about, remember that dreams are among the oldest things in the world.

Would you be so kind as to help me move a tree off my roof? said a man's voice in Sucus's ear.

He woke up and opened his eyes: there was nobody to be seen.

It fell during the storm last night.

Sucus twisted onto his side and saw the talking head of a man in his fifties, going bald, with deep lines across his forehead. The head was in the grass. In front of it, like a lying dog's paws, were a pair of arms. Each elbow was wearing a sort of sandal.

I fear, said the head, that if the wind gets up again, a branch may break a window. If you would care to accompany me?

The speaker had no legs and he advanced by moving his elbows. With each elbow step, his shoulders dragged his body over the grass.

The waste lot ended against a high wall and under this wall stood a large Cadillac without wheels. Its doors were open and, inside, two candles were burning.

On the car roof was a plum tree which had fallen from a terraced garden above.

My problem, said the man, is I can't reach it. I can see it's a plum tree. The wood by daylight is the colour of meat dried by winter wind, so it must be plum. It's gone rotten, it's been eaten, a neglected tree. My problem is, I can't reach it, and even if I got myself onto the hood, I wouldn't have the leverage to pull it off. That's why when I saw you in the grass, so young and strong, I told myself I would take the liberty . . .

Sucus pulled the tree off the car roof. If you had an axe, I'd cut it for you, he said.

An axe I don't have, said the man, but a saw, yes.

Whilst Sucus sawed the small tree into a few logs, the man squirmed about inside the vehicle. A vest was hanging to dry from the steering wheel. Where the passenger's feet would have been was a basin of water. Onto the rearview mirror a picture of the Madonna had been stuck.

I'll open a beer for you when you've finished. It will not, regrettably, be as cold, on such a summer night, as I would wish.

It cuts well, your saw.

Once I used to drive this car, said the man.

The soldiers by the jeeps below were playing with their search light. For a moment its beam picked out the derelict Cadillac. Sucus was leaning on the front wing, drinking from a beer can. The owner lay on his stomach on the back seat.

This is my bed now, he said, smoking a cigarette.

I must go, said Sucus.

I must go . . . That reminds me of my brother, said the man without legs, blowing a smoke ring towards the rear window curtain. My brother is a drinker. At that time he lived in the mountains, rented a house there with his wife. He became close friends with one of his neighbours. They used to shoot clay pigeons together.

I must be going now.

Wait for the end of the story. One evening at the neighbour's house my brother was drinking wine and eating cheese. The neighbour saw how much he liked the cheese, so he left it on the table with another open bottle of wine and told him to enjoy himself to the full, for he, the neighbour, had to go to bed. My brother finished off the bottle, then staggered drunk out of the kitchen and made his way to the bedroom. The neighbour was already asleep. My brother took off his trousers and was about to slip into bed beside the wife. Piss off! she whispered and grabbed his trousers. And she wouldn't give them up. My brother was obliged to go home in his shirt tails!

The storyteller on the back seat rolled over onto his side and started to laugh. He gestured with one hand to his missing legs and, choking with laughter, muttered: Could never explain to his wife where his fucking trousers had gone!

When Sucus got down to the road, a tiny figure beneath the lights on the quayside waved at him. It was Zsuzsa and she was running.

You smell of beer. Are you still hungry? she asked.

My head's turning I'm so hungry.

We're going to eat, she said.

Zsuzsa led Sucus along a narrow street with bright lights and through a door where there was the smell of cooking and the sound of voices, then down some steps into a cellar.

Here we can't run for it, he said.

Don't worry.

A waiter led them to a table.

Do you have calamari? she asked.

Yes, we do.

And goose rillettes?

Yes . . .

Their table was beside an aquarium. Air was being blown in bubbles into the water. The green weeds were waving like hair. Sucus pressed a dirty finger against the glass of the tank. When one of the fish approached, he slid his finger up the glass towards the surface where the bubbles were. The fish, mouth open, gills flickering, followed the finger and swam upwards. Then swiftly Sucus slid it sideways towards Zsuzsa, and the fish followed.

I don't understand, he said.

Aren't you hungry?

I'm starving.

You're going to eat me, Flag, eat me for ever and ever!

water

I f I'm not mistaken, the third of June was Félix's birthday. Félix had an accordion whom he called Caroline. He never married. When he was sixty-two, he fell ill with jaundice and was taken away to the hospital. So he had to sell his seventeen cows; there was nobody to look after them whilst he was in hospital. When he came home, he bought six more. He wouldn't stop, Félix, neither with his cows nor with his music.

The third of June was hot in Troy. When the traffic lights turned red, the waiting drivers hung their arms limply out of their car windows. Only the long cars of the rich were

shut tight, for they were air-conditioned. On the beaches
girls rubbed in suntan lotion every half hour. In the little
workshops of Swansea, an industrial zone of the city, the
cooling fans, set into the brick walls under the metal rooves,
were turning at full tilt, but made the air no cooler. On the
hill of the Escorial the petals, fallen from the magnolia trees,
turned brown. Everywhere the city was grinding the heat
into dust. Yet on Rat Hill Sucus could feel a slight breeze
coming in from the sea.

Zsuzsa's Blue House had two windows with white nylon
curtains. Behind the left-hand curtain was the room where
Zsuzsa's mother—who worked all night—was asleep on a
mattress on the floor. From behind the right hand curtain,
Zsuzsa's younger sister, Julia, was spying on the man her
sister had brought home. He was sitting on a box, his legs
stretched straight out in front of him, his eyes shut, his head
all white with lather. In the doorway of the same house,
leaning against its frame, as if he were a cowboy, stood Zsuzsa's brother, Naisi. Everyone noticed Naisi's boots: calf-
coloured, shining, turned over at the top, they had golden
buckles. His smile was also exceptional. Its cunning was
completely open. His was a cunning, the smile said, which
you could depend upon.

Think it over, said Naisi from the doorway to Sucus on
the wooden box, take your time. There's no point doing a
thing like this if you don't feel comfortable.

Sucus, eyes shut because of the soap, nodded his head.

Zsuzsa came out of the house next door that was made out
of the wood of packing cases with a black bottle in her hand.

What's that? asked Naisi.

Vinegar.

Maybe you should start a hairdresser's, her brother said.

Last week it was a tattooing parlour!

The two go together.

Go together?

Both imply trust, Sister!

Naisi pulled a black handkerchief out of his pocket, flourished it in the air and suspended it over the empty palm of his other hand. Then he began to make the noise of a laying hen. Sucus opened his eyes. Naisi lifted up the black handkerchief to disclose, lying in his palm, a small red packet, tied around a hundred times with white cotton. His hen went quiet.

Crack? asked Sucus.

Naisi laughed, stopped, laughed again, touched his nose and then slipped both packet and handkerchief back into his trouser pockets. Slowly he walked away down the hill towards the tanneries.

Not Naisi's day! said Zsuzsa as she rubbed the soap into Sucus's head. Look at the way he's walking. When he walks like that, he's had bad news.

He just made me a proposition, said Sucus.

Forget it, he's wild when he's skint.

She dug her nails deeper into his scalp and scratched. Sucus's toes curled up with pleasure. She saw them, curled up and splayed out.

Can you do me tomorrow, Miss Crescent Moon? inquired a very old Chinese man with a sunshade who was carrying a bucket of seaweed to his house.

I'm skint too, said Sucus.

We'll go to the Champ-de-Mars and coffee-job together. Later this afternoon, in time for the visits.

No go, said Sucus.

No go why? she asked laughing.

Somebody swiped my thermos this morning.

And the tray?

The tray was in my hands.

I thought you were a jumping cat.

There's this guy who calls out for five glasses, over by the big gate where the soldiers are. He holds up his hand and shouts five. One for each digit, finger, from the Latin *digitus*. So I pour them, put them on the tray and take them across. My back's turned for about thirty seconds. Then this guy pretends he wasn't calling for coffee, he wants tea. I don't have tea. When I get back to my wall I don't have a thermos either! They must have used a kid to snatch it. If I see that guy again he won't last—

We'll get another thermos.

A five-litre thermos, triple insulation, needs a lot of lettuce, and it's hard to find a skanked one.

Then we'll do something else, we'll invent something, Flag.

She scratched harder into his scalp with her silver nails and he moaned with pleasure. This prompted her to soap his neck too, for she wanted to touch the spot she had made the sound come from. Then she rubbed his head more gently till her hands made him drop off.

He was driving along a one-way street. Zsuzsa was the city centre to which the road signs all pointed. But his street was going away from the centre. At the next round-about he read a sign which said: Zsuzsa 638 km.

At this moment she scooped up a basinful of water and threw it over him. The water had been warmed all day by the sun. Sucus scarcely stirred. He just opened his eyes and smiled.

He's very wet, whispered little Julia to herself. She was watching every move through the lace curtains. Her sister got astride the man's legs and sat facing him. He put his hands under her sister's shirt. Her sister was putting her rings back on her fingers; she had taken them off to do the washing.

You could grow me a beard! Zsuzsa whispered to him.

She had found with her fingers the baby in this sturdy man who could carry sacks of cement across his shoulders and whose moustache was like a black aerosol signature saying HOMBRE. Now she wanted to change the baby back into a roused man.

You could grow me a beard, she repeated.

I know a woman with a beard, he replied.

Not for me! For you!

A black beard and the face of a man. And you know what? She has two breasts as large as melons.

So, you've never seen tiny melons?

She keeps an ironmonger's shop. I went there to buy a gas ring for mother. She dropped the old one on the floor and it broke.

And the lady with the beard shows her tits to every customer?

At first I couldn't believe my eyes. She was feeding her baby. She had a beard and a baby! That's how I saw them.

Zsuzsa rested her chin on Flag's wet hair. What makes some hairs straight and others curly? she asked.

In the afternoon heat behind the lace curtains Julia fell asleep. The basin, full of beans she'd been podding, was still on her lap. The flies on the backs of her hands did not wake her.

All the noises on Rat Hill that hot afternoon were drowsy. It was as if no sound had the energy to continue. A chicken cackled and then stopped. A baby cried and went to sleep. Somebody hammered and then the nail was in. A gang of children were playing a game that involved hiding and never being seen or heard. Every dog had found its shade to sleep in. The only continuous noise came from the bottling factory on the Swansea side, a kind of metallic coughing and snoring.

What floor do you live on? Zsuzsa asked.

Fourteenth.

Top storey? Scratch me there again.

No, no, there are twenty-seven floors.

Over Zsuzsa's shoulder Sucus could see the hill opposite, on which the shacks were built so close they almost touched each other. Higher up, the yellowing grass of the hill was criss-crossed by dozens of dust paths so that it looked like an animal losing its fur.

They've got electricity over there?

They got their electricity on Tortoise Hill before we did, she said. We had to wait five years. They built the first houses there the night of the New Year, eighteen months ago. They haven't got water yet. A truck brings it round. Scratch me more there.

You don't need pipes for electricity, Sucus said.

Anyway, they got it before we did.

And here you've got water!

They get less snow in the winter over there than we do here. That's beautiful . . .

So you want to move out?

Depends on you. How many hundred bricks can you lay your hands on? She kissed his eyes.

Millions!

Millions?

Half a dozen.

Holy God! We could build a palace with them. All we need now is a sack of cement.

Use bird-lime!

Wood?

Cut down a tree or two.

Make planks, she said.

Make a bed, he said.

With his fingertips he was playing with the rough hair under her arm, where it was like a nest.

Do we need window frames?

One window to start with, he said.

Take it from a train.

I know where to find a truck chassis, clean, Zsuzsa, not rusty. Five minutes from here. Roof, doors, floor, the lot.

He pressed his elbow into his stomach so he could touch her breasts.

Once, in the presbytery where Monsieur Le Curé Besson lived—he was a man of quiet dignity who drank himself to death—I saw a book, almost as large as the Bible, open at a picture of a young woman offering her breast to an old beggar. The old man had taken the nipple in his toothless mouth and his face was creased in happiness. When Monsieur Le Curé came back into the room, he abruptly closed the book like a shutter on a window. I've never forgotten the picture. If I could find in my blouse the bosom which was once there, two full breasts and their nipples, dear God, for the time it takes to be sucked dry by a child!

Are we going to have a chimney? asked Sucus.

I want mosaics, Flag, like in Santa Barbara.

Blue stones and black jet.

Set in pearl.

She chewed on his wet hair with her teeth.

And ZSUZSA written in gold.

That's right, so the postman knows where to deliver the letters, she said.

Who's going to write?

You, when you go away, you're going to write!

Why do I go away?

To find something else, something you can't find here. You steal a car.

I don't take you in the car?

I wait for you. I cook ful medames all night. And I stay awake praying.

Praying for me to come back.

I'm expecting you back and I'm angry.

I don't come.

I can't believe it.

I have to be rich to come back.

I leave and I start looking for you.

You find me on the day I make twenty million.

So you buy me a panther dress.

And a sapphire ring.

Then we take a ship, Zsuzsa said.

A white ship.

We have a cabin to ourselves.

> In the cabin I tear off your dress.
> I tear off your shirt.
> We're locked in the cabin.
> I've thrown the key away, Flag.

I know why deers fight to the death in the mating season and why they bellow with such a suffering noise. To be male at such a moment is to have a sword thrust between the loins, with its point and half its length protruding. Nothing to do with dreams, not something coiled within. This comes from outside, it skewers the body and it leads him, helpless. It is worse in man than in any other animal because it goes on for longer and it can begin without provocation—as if suddenly a finger in the sky pointed. The sword is pointed too, and double-edged, and along its length it carries its wound. The blade is all the time cutting the wound, and the wound is nothing else but the flesh of the man's little zizi now unrecognisable, because so large and straight. All three of them—man, blade, and zizi—know the same things: that relief cannot come until the sword is plunged into the river it is seeking. Only that river at that moment can heal their wounds, dissolve the sword and make the finger in the sky vanish. We women, rivers of pain and relief.

So Sucus and Zsuzsa embraced, and Julia slept, until Naisi came back up the hill. He was walking slowly and as he walked he kicked at the earth of the path with the toes of his famous calf-coloured boots. The soil was dry and dusty.

When it rained on Rat Hill, the earth was transformed into slides of mud and little rivulets of yellow water that poured down the hillside, like beer down a drenched man's throat. Wet or dry, frozen or baked, the earth on Rat Hill contained fragments and splinters of everything: of glass, brick, china, polystyrene, rubber, earthenware, nails, tin foil, slate, lead, hair, porcelain, zinc, plaster, iron, burnt wood, cardboard, wire, cloth, horn, bone.

Naisi passed the window where his little sister was asleep with the bowl of beans in her lap, he passed the door through which he could see his mother sprawled on the mattress on the floor, and he observed the lovers outside who were kissing with their tongues in each other's mouths.

He stood there alone, and with a voice like the starter of a car that won't catch, hoarse and tired, he said: There's nothing happening today, nothing, nothing, not a fucking thing.

fire

At the moment Zsuzsa's brother Naisi said nothing is happening, not a fucking thing, Clement, Sucus's father, seated on the bed in the two-room flat on the fourteenth floor of the apartment block in Cachan, pressed the ON switch of his television set, which exploded into blue flames. The satin bedspread went up in flames. Clement hurled himself into the kitchen to fetch water, unaware of his burnt face and hands. Only when he picked up an enamel basin in the sink and dropped it as if it were red hot, did he realise he was hurt. His hands felt on fire. He heard Wislawa, his wife, screaming: Jesus! Branch, what have you done to yourself? Branch, what have you done?

White smoke was pouring from the bedroom window. Down below in the street nobody noticed until the first fire engine, hooting like a terrified water bird, rushed through the traffic lights; then people began to look around and eventually to point up at the fourteenth floor. By the time the firemen got their hoses out and extended their ladder, Clement and Wislawa had doused the fire with a bucket and a zinc bath. But Clement had to be taken to hospital in an ambulance. The firemen feared for his eyes.

As a boy he used to sing in the village choir. I loved Clement's voice. When he sang in public he shut his eyes because he did not like being stared at. He stood there, arms at his side, stiff but full of expression. Like a figure carved out of wood. The same forcefulness, the same strength, and the same suffering. Clement left for Troy when he was seventeen. I remember it as if it were yesterday. His older brother, Albert, who was already working as a porter in one of the city's auction rooms, had found him a job. Unfortunately, it did not last long. One day, a few minutes before a large sale was about to start, an auctioneer found Clement asleep on an eighteenth-century four-poster bed which, it was hoped, would realise fifteen million. Naturally, he was sacked on the spot. A few months later he got a job opening oysters and this is what he did for the rest of his life. During the winter he opened oysters and during the summer he loaded fish into refrigerated trucks and railway cars. Sometimes he sang whilst working.

My sheep were grazing
The green mountainside
Tra la la, la la la, la la.

So as not to be sad
To myself I sang
And the echo replied:
Eh oh! eh! oh!

When he was over thirty—and his parents had despaired of him ever getting married—he fell in love with a tally-clerk in a fish warehouse. Her name was Wislawa. She was plump, rosy-complexioned, and she wore thick glasses behind which her eyes were kind and sleepy. Clement was a good dancer. He danced her off her feet. He waltzed like somebody from another century. He also cooked fish for her. He had a way of cooking red gurnards which made them taste like lobster. She watched him with his enormous red hands—always swollen because of the salt water, and painfully cracked because of the ice—preparing the fish on their bed of vegetables and she thought of a mother putting a child to bed, his gestures were so gentle. For her part, she changed his life with a book: a dictionary that explained the origins of words. Clement read it for the next thirty years, and never forgot a thing he learnt. It became a passion. He opened words, as he opened oysters, to find, within, their real meaning. Through words he listened to the past and to what he believed to be the truth. To migrate, from the Latin *migrare*, to change one's abode.

Wislawa's father, a primary school teacher, was outraged when Wislawa told him who she wanted to marry. The fish-monger-son-of-a-peasant! he screamed. Do that, do just that, go on, do it, and ruin my life! And my life! she said very quietly and with great determination, for Wislawa, because of her poor health, knew exactly what she wanted. Clement, large, quiet, wooden, was to be the tree of her life: in him she would perch. And perch she did.

Clement brought Wislawa to the village for the wedding. I was there. During the next few years they sometimes came back on visits—particularly in July so they could help Clement's parents, Casimir and Angeline, bring in the hay. Casimir was the brother of Marcel, the Marcel who went to prison for kidnapping the two government inspectors. Each time Clement and Wislawa arrived, Casimir made a point of tentatively placing his hand on her belly even before embracing his son. Yet the years passed and his daughter-in-law was never pregnant.

Then one July he put his hand on her stomach and was as usual shaking his head, when she nodded. No? he said, incredulous. Yes! she said and laughed. Let me get my thingamebob, lie down on the table and close your eyes. Casimir came back with a tiny chain attached to a wedding ring. Holding the end of the chain between his finger and thumb, he let the ring hang suspended over her magnificent belly. Wislawa couldn't stop laughing. Angeline held her hand to calm her. The ring started to move and then to swing out in ever-widening circles. It's a boy! cried Casimir, a grandson!

The child was conceived at Easter, said Wislawa, at least I think so.

You mean in this house on your last visit! shouted Casimir triumphantly.

I think so.

We gave them our bed, Angeline, you remember?

So we did.

He was conceived in this house, cried Casimir, and in our bed! He belongs here! He's our man . . . And he embraced his son and then his daughter-in-law.

Let us drink to HIM and his mother! In the cellar I have a bottle that I have kept for half a century, just for this occasion! Ah, my dear Clement, what a happiness a son is . . .

The thingamebob was right. Wislawa was carrying a boy. Sucus was born the following January, under the sign of Aquarius, the Water-Carrier.

From Troy they were always promising to come back to the village to show Casimir and Angeline their grandson, but, after the birth, Wislawa's health got worse and Clement's earnings became feebler and feebler as prices in Troy increased a hundredfold. So they put off coming and both grandparents died without ever having seen their grandson. The years passed and Clement taught Sucus all that he knew about the truth of words.

So you've come, my son, said Clement from the hospital bed.

Yes, Papa.

Come to see me for the last time, eh?

Why do you say last?

Do you know how long I've been here now? Eight days! You look better.

The lift's too small to take coffins, they tell me. They'll have to carry mine down the stairs. How's your mother?

All right.

Stop staring at me.

You'll get better, Papa.

They won't let me see myself in a mirror. The man-over-there's wife came to visit him, so I asked her if she had one in her handbag. When she held out the mirror to me, her hand was trembling.

Maybe it always trembles. Maybe it's a disease that makes her hand tremble.

Shh! He may hear you. He's not deaf.

Maybe there's no cure for her trembling. Who knows?

You know everything, don't you!

He wasn't burnt like you? asked Sucus.

He's badly concussed. Concussion.

Something fell on him?

Worse, son, it was an icon. He's Russian and thinks it was a punishment sent by God. Retribution. From the Latin *retribuere*, to pay back, from *tribuere*, to pay, originally to share out among the *tribes*. You see what that means? In *retribution* there's still the tribe, the clan, where we came from.

What did he do wrong?

He hasn't told me.

The Russian in the next bed opened his eyes. There's a Russian proverb, he said, When you cut down trees, the chips fly. He shut his eyes again and added, One of them fell on my head.

This silenced all three men. Further along the ward a man was calling for a nurse. His voice was broken; the self-respect gone.

Sucus couldn't take his eyes off his father's face. It was burnt all over, as brown as a chicken left too long in the oven. A brown crust had smoothed over the pouches of the face. More than this, it hid the lines and wrinkles, and disguised the dome of the forehead where his father was going bald. The marks of strain and effort, pain and tear, had been burnt away. The blue eyes, peering through the two narrow judas slits, and his pink tongue, were those of a young man.

I looked at the burnt-out TV, Sucus said.

It was faulty wiring.

You were lucky.

The truth about those machines, and it's the same everywhere today, everywhere you turn you find monkey work. We called it monkey work, son, in the village.

So you've been telling me for twenty years. But assembling TV sets isn't like opening oysters.

Shut your mouth.

His huge bandaged hands were lying on the bedspread and looked bigger than ever.

Insert the point of the knife! Crack! said Sucus. Cut round the frill. Sever the nerve. And there's your oyster! One operation. What I don't understand is why it suddenly went Phut! It wasn't as if it was a new one.

Faulty wiring. And faulty wiring means monkey work. Incompetence. From *competere*, in Latin to compete, from *cum*, with, and *petere*, to go towards. To go somewhere together, son. There are so few places to go to now. *In*competence, to go nowhere, to be with nobody. To do monkey work.

After speaking, Clement laid his head back on the pillow. He was having some difficulty in breathing.

Your mother and I have tried to do our best for you, he said. Inculcate certain principles.

In-cul-cate, said Sucus, from the Latin *inculcare*, to tread upon.

Over the iron frame of the bed, above Clement's head, was draped a scarf with blue gentians on a green ground. Wislawa had brought it for him on the first day. She had a whole collection of scarves. Many of them she pinned over the walls of the kitchen at home to hide the damp stains. This gave the tiny room on the fourteenth floor the look of a fortune teller's caravan. Now, in the hospital ward, he rubbed the back of his bandaged hand against the gentians. After a moment he spoke again and opened his eyes.

When you've opened a million oysters, every oyster on this earth is the same. I started near the Opera, my boy. I worked for a man who said he'd been a sailor. In any case, he wore a sailor's hat. He looked at my hands and said, They're big enough, you'll do.

Why should it suddenly go Phut?

Because my hour had come.

Phut! Phut!

You believe in nothing!

You'll get better!

When your hour strikes, there's nothing to be done.

Nothing to be done! One minute you're accusing the women who assemble your TV of monkey work—

Women?

Sure, it's all done by women.

The monkey work?

You didn't know it was done by women, did you?

I never thought about it.

It's their fingers.

I've lost the feeling in my hands. So they're all put together by women?

Yes, put together by women. And the next moment you're talking about fate and your fucking hour striking.

What do you mean by their fingers?

Nimble. Women have nimble fingers.

You've always been the same, Sucus.

Clement succeeded in doing what he wanted with the scarf. With his two bound hands he pulled it off the bars of the bed and held it against his cheek.

I stayed with the sailor by the Opera for a year. I learnt the trade. You weren't even thought of. Then I started on my own. Now it's all over.

Don't talk like that.

I've always tried to be philosophical. *Philo*, love of, *sophos*, wisdom. Open the drawer. Clement indicated the locker beside the bed. I want you to have the knife.

Inside was an identity card, blue like the colour of the Trojan sky before the traffic begins on a summer morning, its corners dog-eared, its edges frayed, its code number of three letters and eight numerals too faint for anyone to read, a cigarette lighter, a key ring, a bottle opener, and a fisherman's knife with a handle made of reindeer horn.

You know it, son, so take it.

Sucus took it out of the drawer and examined the handle.

Yes, I know it, he said obediently, and here's the mark the knifemaker made because it was no ordinary reindeer.

Now you must pay me, said Clement, a knife can only be sold.

How much?

Ten.

Sucus laughed. They don't exist any more, Papa, ten pieces! The smallest coin now is a hundred.

Then give me a hundred.

Sucus searched in the pockets of his jeans. I haven't got a sou.

So pay me tomorrow, Sucus, and never use it against a man unless he threatens your life.

Sucus noticed that in the corners of his father's mouth a little white foam was collecting.

I'll sell it back to you when you're better, he said, for five hundred!

One day your hour will strike too. Take the knife.

All this because a TV goes phut!

My hour has struck.

I've brought you some gnôle.

Pass it here, son, under the cover. Have you found a job yet?

There are no jobs, said Sucus, except the ones we invent. No jobs. No jobs.

Clement couldn't hold the bottle to his mouth with his hands, so Sucus held it for him.

It was the first time Sucus had been in a hospital. Nothing in the ward or in the ablutions or in the corridors, whether it was flesh or metal, remained unwashed for more than a few days; the ward smelt of soap and its powerlessness against the afflictions of age.

Take a mouthful, Sucus. Plum brandy. *Prunum*. Slivovitz. Go back to the village, that's what I'd like to do.

It's thousands of miles away.

See the mountains for the last time.

Are you serious?

I'll never see the village again. I'll never set eyes on it again. There are people, I'm sure, who drive through it, without even noticing it.

When you're better—

Listen to the name of our village! It means lucky-horse-with-a-broken-leg.

It always sounded like nonsense to me.

To you it would, Sucus. There's only you who makes sense, according to you. In this sad wide world there's only you. The rest of us are fools who know nothing.

Tell me how you think it can be lucky to have a busted leg!

When I was fifteen I was looking after four hundred sheep.

How's it lucky to have a broken leg?

If your horse breaks a leg, you have to stay where you are. So?

That's how our village was founded centuries ago.

And what was so good about that?

I've thought about it. I've given the matter some thought. They came from the south over the mountains.

Why not from the lake to the west?

It would have been summer, like now. They had some difficulty fording the river. They wanted to cross to the sunny side.

What you call the *adret*—

So you do remember some things! Yes, the *adret*. I think they would have tried to cross by Sous-Chataigne, where the old man Digue lived. He drank five litres a day and could carry a mare on his back. Yet when he grew old, like me now, he couldn't move out of his chair, poor man, and when he spoke, people told him, Careful what you're saying, Digue, and don't exaggerate! They would have tried to cross by Sous-Chataigne; it's the shallowest reach of the river. The chief was in the lead, picking his way, and his horse slipped on the boulders and broke a leg. Foreleg, I'd say, wouldn't you?

Right foreleg, I'd say, Papa.

So the man gave the order: Pitch camp here tonight. And they stayed. They never struck camp again. They discovered the valley, the green valley they were dreaming of. They found it good. They built houses on the *adret*, where the church now is.

A nurse walked down the aisle between the beds of infirm and wounded men, half of whom were remembering their villages or their mothers. Sucus hid the bottle. The nurse changed Clement's drip-feed. When she'd gone, Clement whispered to Sucus.

Give me another gulp . . . My old friend Dédé, he's from the village and I was talking to him about you last month. He's with a building firm these days, he said he might be able to help. They've opened a new site on Park Avenue. They need to hire men. He said you should ask for a man named Cato and say you came from Dédé. Promise me you'll try.

It'll be too late by now.

Who knows? I want you to promise.

And supposing the horse had broken its fucking leg in some other place?

Then we wouldn't be here!

You don't think somebody a bit like me, Papa, might have slipped out somehow?

Clement shut his eyes and his hands felt for the gentian scarf.

I wouldn't be here, nor would you.

So here we are in this goddamned Troy without jobs. Here we are in the month of July. And you want me to stand up and say thank you for a horse's broken leg a thousand years ago. Thanks to his leg—no, thanks to his broken leg we're drinking gnôle!

That's history, son. Clement didn't open his eyes.

And what we live now is what? asked his son.

Don't ask me. I don't know. It's not history. It's a kind of waiting. His bandaged hands were clenching the scarf.

I know a man who works at Budapest Station, said Sucus. When you're better maybe he could fit you into a freight car. How many days would it take to go back, Papa?

With you! Clement's eyes were still shut: the judas slits

were still closed. I want to show my village to you, my son. I want to show you the house where I was born, the church where your mother and I got married, the chapel where Jean seduced the Cocadrille, the factory where they make molybdenum, the pass of St. Pair where the ravens fly, the blueberries and the bolets . . . Promise me, Sucus?

What do you want me to promise?

Promise me!

I'm afraid you must leave now, said a nurse, visiting hours are over.

Promise me to go to Park Avenue, whispered his father, and bit his under lip.

Sucus walked down the aisle between the hundred beds and made for the door. The white bedspreads were all identical, and each one was pulled over a distinct pain. Sucus thought the helplessness of the men under the covers was worse than their pain. I don't want to live to be more than forty, he told himself. By then Sucus will have done all he wants. When I'm forty, before Sucus gets to this, I'm going to see Sucus dies. Then he thought of Zsuzsa and her arse, and he thought of where his hand felt under and behind her, and where there was no end to her.

The thought made him hurry. He took the stairs three at a time and was out of the building before he knew it. Several beggars stood on the hospital steps, hands extended. He paused before one. May merciful Heaven bless you and give you what you need, the white-haired man mumbled. Sucus leapt down the remaining steps.

Pig's Runt! the beggar spat after him.

On the pavement a woman was selling flowers and a man, pretzels. The flowers were red as blood and the pretzels smelt of kitchens. Without hesitating he stepped off the pavement and ran into the six lanes of traffic. Suddenly, between two coaches, he turned round and ran back, past the vendors on the pavement, up the steps, towards the hospital. There was a crush of people round the main entrance, so he made for a side door. There he found himself face to face with a lion.

The lion was waiting for him. Sucus put out his hand to touch the lion's mane, and came to his senses. The life-size animal, carved from lion-coloured marble, was only a few centimetres thick and in low relief. The arch behind the lion, the vaulting, the passageway, the tiles along the floor, the door at the end, all were false; they had all been made to deceive and to please when the building was a palace.

Trembling, he pushed his way through the crush around the main entrance and rushed up the stairs to the ward where he had left his father.

Clement's bed was surrounded by screens. Even from far off Sucus knew it was his father's bed. There were some people behind the screens. He could see their feet. One man and two nurses in stockings.

What's happening? he asked.

He's gone, said the Russian.

Clement is standing before me. He is wearing the coat of bees. It is as warm as bearskin and as thick. But like any swarm, it is alive. The bees, unlike the bear, are not dead. They are calm, sweet-tempered, rather quiet, but they are alive, moving, vibrating and concentrated on their queen. It is a perfect fit, in the form of a pilot's jacket, tight round the neck and sleeves and waist, and full across the chest and shoulders. Black flecked with orange. From far away, you'd say an Irish tweed. Close up, the flickering of every bee is visible. Clement loosens the collar. Then, clenching lightly the fingers of his hand, he pulls an arm out of one of the sleeves. I step forward to help him. I hold the shoulders so he can withdraw his second arm. Not a single bee is crushed and, naturally, not a single bee flies away. The coat is murmuring too. This is the only thing that has changed. The murmur of the bees has grown louder. I hang the coat on the branch of a plum tree. Bees love the smell of its leaves. I smooth the hair round Clement's big ears. So I've come, he says.

One of the nurses in the public ward of the hospital for the poor came out from behind the screen. She had the severe face of somebody who has given many years of her life to charity, who has struggled night after night, alone, with indifference.

Who are you? she asked Sucus.

I'm the son. He was my father.

I'm afraid I have to tell you, young man—

I know—he's gone!

Behind her he could see the male porter in a white coat and the other nurse. They were lifting something up.

Would you like to come with me to the office?

He ran. Between the beds, down the stairs and out of the building. He ran faster than the first time. He did not stop to look at the beggars or the flower-seller. His one idea was to get to Cachan. He turned left out of the hospital. He took the Boulevard Cantor. He turned down Kibalchich Street. He crossed Lions. He went over the Hind Bridge. He passed by Swansea and he came into Cachan High Street by the

Réaumur Monument. It was only in the lift, going up to the fourteenth floor, that he found the words with which he would break the news to Wislawa. The once blue walls of the lift were covered from floor to ceiling with drawings, initials, names, dates scratched into the paint. There was a drawing of a prick he'd done when he was ten. He took out his father's knife and scratched in capital letters the word PHUT. And in order to finish it, he went up to the twentieth floor and came down again to the fourteenth.

When people die here they are all buried in the village cemetery. With time, their names, cut in marble, are effaced by the frost, the sun, and the rain; eventually they are forgotten, as the dead have been from the beginning. Yet, nameless, they are still remembered in the course a road follows, in the placing of a bridge over a river, in the way a wall runs, in the paths that lead over the mountains. In Troy it is different. There the names of the dead are forgotten more quickly. The only ones remembered are those with streets named after them. Otherwise, millions disappear without trace, leaving behind no landmark. In the city the bereaved alone carry their dead in their heads. The only memorials are private choices. Here we have so few choices. In Troy they need the dead to help them, because they face so many.

As Sucus was putting his key into the door, Wislawa opened it. Behind her was their kitchen, its walls covered in scarves.

He's left us both, Mother. Father died.

She stared at him and time stopped for them both as they stood in the doorway. They did not want anything to continue, for each of them knew that the pain would only begin when they came back. So they let the echo of the words go on and on, till finally it disappeared into timelessness.

Then Sucus shut the door and Wislawa fell to her knees. Her jaw was thrust out in determination. It was as though the cruelty of the event had entered her and settled on her face. She bit down on her chin with her teeth. Still kneeling, she slumped forward so as to be able to crawl on all fours. Like this she went into the bedroom. Once, before the fire, there had been a wall-to-wall carpet on the floor, now it was bare cement. With her hand she plucked at the cement as if picking one flower after another from grass.

Oh, Branch, she whispered, how can we manage with what they've done to you, darling? Tell me! Tell me!

concrete

Today I went into the stable because I heard one of them kicking. They play me up these days, they piss in the hay that I give them, they jump into their mangers, they butt, just like goats do every year at Easter. And there she was, when I opened the stable door, there she was my black one, as wide as she was long, flanks extended, her four feet placed together on one small spot, and she was pushing hard, neck outstretched, head down, and, at her other end, the snout of her belly rooting the air and gaping, with the cabri's head already out. I pulled his front paws, warm and sticky with love, and he came into my hands as easily as a slipper comes off a foot. He weighed a good eight kilos and he was brown and white. In two minutes he was on his four feet, he stuck out his long ears sideways as if they were a pole that would help him balance, and he made his first leap. Cabris are born in the air. Meanwhile, the mother, who was about to push out the second kid, but in her own time, turned her good-for-nothing head and looked at me with her oblong black pupils which hide all expression except that of a distant and insolent curiosity. She looked at me long and hard. What will happen next, she asked, not to you and your broom and your shovel and your stool, but to me? Her udder was as full as a bell is with sounds. The stump of his horns, I told her, which I can feel with my fingers on his head, will grow, and he'll walk on his hind legs trying to eat the moon.

It was early morning in Troy. A man was climbing up thin metal rungs inside a narrow tower scarcely wider than his shoulders. The tower was transparent, its walls made of air. The ladder was absolutely vertical. The man in his blue working clothes was almost invisible against the blue sky. He had a large black moustache which his daughter, Chrysanthe, liked to outline with her forefinger. It's a crow flying! she would cry. The man's name was Yannis. In the bag over his shoulder as he climbed up into the sky was some bread, a slice of lamb, and a carton of orange juice.

There is a moment early in the morning before much blood has been spilt, before the pitilessness of the strong has reached its apogee, when the night players are at last asleep and free of their sadness, there is a moment when the new day seems almost innocent.

To take food up to the crane was strictly forbidden, for it was thought to encourage the drinking of alcohol. Yannis, however, was a man who did what he wanted and ignored

other people's rules. If they could find a better operator than
he, let them find one!

Below him, the cars driving along Park Avenue were moving slowly in both directions, and were so close together that
the traffic lanes in the early morning sunshine looked like
metal snake toys. On the flat roof of the police station on
Cauchy Street, three policemen in track suits were doing
exercises.

At the top of the tower Yannis stepped out onto the perforated platform before his cabin. He liked to eat his breakfast
alone in the sky. It gave him the chance to question leisurely.

How was he to get rid of the cockroaches that had invaded
his flat? They came out every night, and twice his two daughters had woken up screaming that the beasts had got into
their hair.

A wind came off the sea, and white clouds were being
blown northwards like cotton flowers. Gently, securely, the
crane rocked.

The problem with the cockroaches was that Yannis could
not stand the smell of ammonia. It gave him a migraine. Yet
everyone swore ammonia was the only cure. Murat the Turk
claimed there was a powder you could use against cockroaches, which had no smell. He must ask him the name.

Yannis was the operator of the father crane. Large construction sites in Troy used two jib cranes. The father was
always ten or so metres taller than the mother, with a longer
arm. Her arm could pass beneath his. Thus, when the two
were delivering at the same time, they could feed the same
area without their booms touching.

Eating his breakfast in the sky, Yannis wrote a postcard
to his mother:

Happy Birthday, Maman. In a few weeks I'll be sending

an air ticket. You will fly across the wine-dark sea. I'll be at the airport to meet you. You'll live in our apartment. Chrysanthe and Daphine are longing to meet their grandmother. I'll take you across the New Bridge—look on the other side of this card—to the great church of Santa Barbara. Sonia is expecting a child in November! Perhaps a grandson this time. I'm writing this in my crane.

Far below, in the direction of his left foot, a group of workers in yellow helmets were drinking coffee out of cardboard cups. One of them was Sucus. They were sitting in the shade of an archway, which, long before, had been the entrance to the city's silver market. The day was not yet hot. Some of the men were wearing shorts, their legs brown as camels.

The Greek up there is smart, one of them told Sucus, he can get his motherfucking crane, which lifts forty tons, to pull a cork out of a bottle!

I wasn't born yesterday, said Sucus.

Newborn wasn't born yesterday! said a man with a red handkerchief round his neck.

So he doesn't believe us! said another who had stuck onto his helmet a pin-up of a woman with naked breasts like cumulus clouds.

Hey, Newborn! How long can you hold a litre at arm's length—like this?

As long as you.

How many minutes?

Seven, eight.

If you make it for five, we'll pay your beer at lunch.

Give me the bottle.

If you don't make it, you pay for our beer, said the man with the goddess helmet.

For all of you!

Yep. All of us.

It's just water, ordinary water?

City water, man. One kilo plus the bottle.

Where's the trick?

Newborn thinks there's a trick. There's nothing tricky here. You don't stop, that's all. You hold it up. For five minutes.

Which hand?

Any hand you like. Hold it straight.

Who's got a watch?

Okay. Start.

Sucus, on his feet, held the bottle in his right hand, arm outstretched sideways, straight from the shoulder, like a crane.

One minute!

Sucus clutched the bottle a little harder.

Two!

Newborn says he's going to keep it there for seven minutes.

He could feel the shape of the muscle in his shoulder, and its hardness, growing bigger like a stone in a fruit.

Three minutes.

Now it hurt. Not the weight. The weight was nothing. It was the stone in his shoulder insisting that it be moved. He twisted his head a little to squint along his arm.

He's not going to make it.

On the spreader beam of the mother crane, hanging from its two cables, Sucus read over and over again the words: THINK SAFETY. THINK SAFETY. Everything he thought passed so quickly, leaving behind empty seconds which were wordless.

All the men were watching his puckered, red face.

A swallow flew into the roof of the archway above. For a split second Sucus glanced up to find it. He recognised a nest, the colour of cement.

Swallows, two wings carrying a soul, that's why they fly so fast, his father used to say.

Four minutes!

The question of pain counted no more. It was a question of how to keep the arm in the air. Nothing was holding it up except a thought. The thought was one word, endlessly repeated: UP!

Newborn's going to keel over!

He'll break the bottle!

Look at him!

Five minutes! whispered the man with the goddess helmet, he's won!

Sucus still kept the bottle up.

Five and a half minutes!

The men watched now without any expectation but more intently than before. The excitement of the wager over, curiosity remained and wanted nothing to stop. The exploit had become mildly surprising and they were happy to suck between their teeth the sweetness of this surprise.

Sucus didn't know it, but he was saying UUPP out loud.

Six minutes, Newborn!

Murat the Turk with whom Sucus worked on the concrete mixer, clambered to his feet, walked over to Sucus, and put the palm of his hand gently under the bottom of the bottle to take its weight.

Your victory! he said so softly the others didn't hear him.

Sucus opened his eyes and stared at Murat. Murat wore his yellow helmet low over his brow. With his right hand he was eating an apple and on his left he still wore an industrial glove.

. . .

Back to work, cried the man with the goddess helmet, Cato's out of his hotel!

Cato, the personnel manager on the site, ate his breakfast alone in a hut that had framed pictures on its walls. He drove to work in a Volvo. A short man, he was as bald as an egg when he took off his yellow helmet. The helmets were regulation issue to everybody and wearing them was compulsory. Those worn by the workers were mostly chipped and dented, those worn by visiting architects, or representatives of the Mond Bank, for whom the building was being built, were immaculate. Cato had deliberately chosen for himself the most battered helmet he could find. There was no yellow paint left on it. In his view his chosen helmet showed he was the toughest man around.

To operate his crane Yannis needed to move no more than I do embroidering a baby's bib. In each hand he had a red keyboard with black buttons, and he sat on his throne like a judge. He looked down through the glass front of his cabin. Cato was giving orders and the men were going back to work, so he turned eastwards, towards the morning sun and the concrete mixer. The jib rode the air like a cormorant.

The concrete mixer was the kitchen of the construction site. The cement was stored in two cannisters, each one as tall as a house. Cement needs to be kept as dry as flour. Beneath the cannisters was a mixing bin into which the cement ran according to the measure decided. Murat commanded the measures on an electronic control panel. The amounts depended upon the destination of the concrete. Murat had worked for three years on cement mixers. He knew them and their pitfalls as well as a priest knows the catechism.

From the bin beneath the cannisters the mix was conveyed on a belt into the drum. Inside this great rotating drum, water fell onto the dry mix and turned it into feed. The rotation was clockwise until the moment when Murat needed to fill a hopper. Then he reversed the motor and the great drum turned counterclockwise, so its metal tongues lolled sideways and the batch slipped out.

When Murat wanted to show Yannis in the sky that the hopper was full, he removed his yellow helmet and raised it above his head. Yannis immediately took up the weight and lifted the hopper a few centimetres off the earth. Then, pressing the black buttons, he nudged the hoist-crab, which ran on lines along the jib, he nudged it a few centimetres forward and abruptly a few centimetres backwards. The resulting jolt set the hopper and the cables swinging. When they swung away from the drum, he hauled the load up. Like this, the hopper as it left the ground never grazed the drum's nose. When it was clear, Murat made a sign as if he were throwing a bird into the sky, and the hopper soared high into the air, dripping its grey rain.

Sucus was shovelling towards the grabs, which worked like a dredger taking the ballast to the bin for the mix. The evening before, a truck driver who was in despair because his son had died of meningitis, had dumped a load of gravel far away from the grabs and driven off without a glance, crying Jesus! Jesus!

Get this lot moved! Cato had told Sucus.

Might be quicker with a calfdozer.

Dozer, my arse!

Sucus straightened his back and watched the hopper in the sky as it circled the site. The sun was higher and the morning was getting hot. He took off his vest. His skin was paler than that of the other men because he was new to the work.

I remember the pale skin of peasants and soldiers on the rare occasions when they strip. Its whiteness is meant for the night not the day, for our beds not the fields.

Construction, from the Latin *struere*, to heap, *con struere*, to heap together. Sucus shovelled the gravel. When he straightened his back and paused he had a habit of touching his moustache with three fingers of his right hand. Murat strolled over to the heap, and the two men stood side by side, wordless, savouring their idleness, wiping the dust off their lips.

Like shifting a bloody mountain, Sucus eventually said.

If you do the bottle trick again, I'll tell you the secret, said Murat. You have to imagine you're walking. Shut your eyes, walk home to your house and remember everything you pass and everything you see when you arrive! It's all in here. He tapped his yellow helmet. The whole world's in here! Just imagine you're walking home instead of standing still! Like that you can hold the weight for ten minutes.

Sucus spat on his palms and shovelled again. The task came to his aid. Tasks do this sometimes. They lift the shovel, loosen the earth, hold the nail straight, direct the axe, balance the load across the shoulders. Above all, they make themselves look small. They cease to be gigantic. They divide themselves up. Each time you straighten your back and take a breath, another small part of the task has been accomplished.

Finally the noon whistle sounded.

.   .   .

When Zsuzsa approached the old arch to the silver market, the eating stopped. Barefoot, she was wearing a dress, pale blue with a long skirt and short tight sleeves. Cato peered through the window of his hut. She was an unauthorised person, but considering the twenty mesmerised men, he decided to say nothing for once.

Hi! sweetheart, shouted the man with the red handkerchief, his knife, with cheese on it, still in midair.

I'm looking for Flag. Does he work here?

Flag? We don't know any Flag, do we? How long has he been here?

He's been working here for a week now.

Ah. She means Newborn. I saw him a minute ago. Come and sit down. He'll be back. Have some beer. Where are you from?

Not from here.

Not from here she says. Who's from here? Do you know how elephants hide, beautiful?

Behind jokes like yours! said the man with the goddess helmet.

No. They put on glasses.

God help us!

Well, have you ever seen an elephant wearing glasses?

Let her sit down on the box there.

You haven't, have you? Which only goes to show, doesn't it, if they're wearing glasses, elephants are invisible!

Zsuzsa sat on the box as if she were sitting in a train, idly looking out of the window.

Did Newborn know you were coming? asked Murat.

No, it's a surprise.

If we all had a surprise like you! said the goddess man.

At this moment Sucus arrived, running.

You look daft in that helmet, Flag. Why do you all eat with your helmets on?

Safety regulations. Bet you have some too?

Several of the men laughed. Sucus took off his helmet and led her away from them.

.   .   .

Do you like my earrings? she asked.

They were gold-coloured and each one was large enough to pass a lemon through. When she moved, they tilted like dwarf cart wheels.

Not bad.

And my blue dress?

Yes.

I wanted to impress you.

You have! Who gave you the earrings?

So, it's going to be twenty storeys high, your building!

She looked up at the cranes, and whilst her head was back, he kissed her throat.

Who did?

Did what?

Gave you the earrings?

My ears were pierced when I was three. My grandmother pierced them. So I have to wear earrings. It follows, doesn't it?

Who was it?

You're jealous, Flag! Jealous!

How did you get them?

You'd do better to think of your poor father.

He's dead.

All of us are going to die one day, Flag. I wear jewelry so everybody can see we're alive. Me and them. And I want you to make me a promise.

What?

When I die I want you to see I'm wearing earrings in my coffin! If I'm not wearing them, you must thread them on my ears. Promise me you'll do that!

She looked again at the cranes.

Have you been up there in the sky? It must be great up there in the crane—like God.

Who gave them to you?

Perhaps I nicked them.

You did!

I didn't. You want to hit me, do you, Flag?

Yes.

Go on then, hit!

No.

Hit me!

Fuck you!

I win! I've made you angry! Here take them.

Are they gold? asked Sucus, examining them.

Yes, they're gold.

Was it a man who gave them to you?

You really want to know? Well, I nicked them.

You said you didn't.

They're gold. You haven't given me anything made of gold, Flag!

She was jeering at him.

Aiee! Now you hit me! Give them to me.

Don't say that again!

I want you to give them to me.

Sucus held out the earrings on the palm of his cement-coloured hand. They weighed nothing and yet he could feel their warmth.

Give me the earrings. Now it's you who's given them to me. And now because it's you who's given them to me, Flag, I'll never take them off for anyone.

With one side of her face flushed where Sucus had slapped her, Zsuzsa started to dance, beside a stack twice as tall as her of rusty grills used for reinforcing the concrete.

I can't remember when I first saw it, it was too long ago. It belongs to the high mountains which the snow never leaves. It happens at the height of the glaciers, often on them, but never at a lower altitude. It has always reminded me of heaven. The sunlight catches the snow and instead of making it blinding white, it makes it glisten. It's a molten light and it comes and goes and changes place, measuring the sun as no instrument can. For this light to occur, snow crystals have to melt into moisture and then freeze again as hard as enamel, and then melt and be frozen again. In this light coming off the ice there is a warmth and a trace of sugar as in a mother's milk. And when Zsuzsa danced beside the stack of rusty grills, the arms of her dress stained with sweat, and her mouth open because she was laughing, her teeth with their two gaps glistened with this light.

Suddenly she stopped and let her arms fall to her sides.

You must look after your mother, Flag. She needs you these days.

She started to dance again, this time slowly, throwing out one arm to one side and then the other to the other, like a man sowing seeds with two hands.

There was no way round her, Sucus thought, following her every movement. You could turn your back and walk away, but if you took one step forward, you had to go through her. Even if you went way out to the side, it would still be through her. Wherever you went she got there first. She must have been the same all her life, from the time she could first stand on her two legs. Everything she could see here— the cement dust, the crane, the rusty grills, the sky, Murat, the other men watching—everything she could see, everything that passed by, everything that rose and fell, was Zsuzsa, and was part of her, not of something else. This was why there was no way round her.

She stopped dancing and brushed the cement dust off her feet.

We'll buy your mother some fish tonight, some fresh gurnards, I'm sure she likes red gurnards, doesn't she?

The whistle sounded.

Five fucking minutes early, said the goddess helmet.

Cato sounds it when he wants!

Zsuzsa walked away along the edge of the road the trucks took to bring in the sand and gravel. The driver, who had lost his child the day before, did not notice whether she was a man or woman: she was simply another figure on the road to be avoided.

Yannis, going to his crane, tapped Sucus on the shoulder and told him:

At home when a young woman dances alone, we say she's asking for a husband!

Far away, your home! said Sucus.

No, my friend, women don't change. She was dancing for you.

The whistle sounded again.

.   .   .

Hose down her gutters! said Murat to Sucus, nodding at an empty hopper. The water that dripped from the nozzle of the hose made a blister on Sucus's hand smart. The force of the jet he directed against the hopper knocked off the crumbs of drying concrete.

Yannis climbed up to his cabin in the sky. The first job of the afternoon was to deliver four shutterings, complete with scaffolding and bridges, to the south. When not being used, all the shutterings were kept in the north. Stacked together, grey with cement, they made a block like a bunker. Yet when hammered they rang out like metal. Yannis swung his crane over the mother's arm, northwards, and whilst swinging he ran out the crab and lowered the cables. It took a little time to attach the chains and loop them to the cable hooks, so he let his eyes wander to the sea where the ships passed. Whenever he looked at the sea he dreamt of returning home.

A rigger, far below, raised his hands, joined as if in prayer, to heaven. This was the sign for Yannis to hoist. The giant metal shuttering, which would hold the concrete feed until it solidified into a wall, left the ground. Yannis turned the crane like the hour hand of an immense clock, over the sheds, the archway, the wasteland where Zsuzsa danced, the central blocks, to the southernmost point of its orbit. The top of the crane's mast, as it carried the load, rocked, predictably, like a tree top. Only Yannis's eyes were fixed.

With the tips of his fingers on the black buttons, he had to place twelve tons of metal as gently as Gabriel placed his words at the Annunciation. Slowly, he let the cables run out. He brought the crab back a bare twenty centimetres. Continued lowering. Then stopped to take off his sunglasses. He let the cables run again. The cabin tilted forward as if it too were anxious to see, and, far below, ten workers the size of bees manhandled the massive shuttering, still afloat on the summer air, into its exact position, exact enough for every bolt to drop into its hole.

Bull! shouted one of them and lowered his outstretched arms. Yannis let the cables go slack. The shuttering rested on its own weight. Twelve tons.

. . .

You, Newborn, ever think about justice? asked Murat.

I keep away from the law.

We're not talking about their justice.

Whose then?

I'm talking about what happens to us.

You all say *us* when you start to get old. I talk about me. Who's us?

Every day the law of the funnel spreads further and further, said Murat.

What's the law of the funnel?

The funnel of wealth, Newborn, it's broad for some and narrow for others.

A hopper came down to be filled. Sucus pushed it up against the drum.

Bull! shouted Murat and lowered his outstretched arms.

Nobody could any longer remember how the shouted word *bull* had come to mean *slacken, in place, home!* It was a kind of oath. The crane drivers could rarely hear it and they depended for their manoeuvres on manual signs and the evidence of their own eyes. The oath was simultaneously a curse and a mute plea.

The giant drum turned counterclockwise, its tongues lolled sideways, the feed came out.

Murat took off his helmet and lifted it into the air. The hopper with its grey rain rose higher than small birds fly.

You've never imagined the world different? asked Murat.

Yes, maybe they'll blow it up.

And us with it.

So where's your justice? demanded Sucus looking hard into Murat's calm black eyes.

Take a baby's hands, said Murat, wiping his forehead with the back of his glove, they're so delicate, so well made. Their nails are like tiny rose petals, each finger able to move by itself. Perfectly made fists, the size of apricots! Why are baby's hands like that?

I don't know.

Made for what?

Wiping up crap.

No, for taking what belongs to us.

Nothing belongs to us.

One day it will.

Never.

Murat threw a tiny switch and another measure of cement fell into the mixing bin.

If we keep the idea of justice alive under our yellow helmets, Murat said, if we all keep it alive together, one day the world will belong to us.

You're a dreamer like my dad was.

So why are baby's hands so well made?

I don't know.

Now Murat threw the switches for the gravel and sand.

What union was your father in?

He wasn't.

You said he was a dreamer.

My father dreamt of the village he left, and you, you dream of the future. Meanwhile we're here, you and I are here, mixing concrete here for the Mond Bank.

A shadow moved over the earth. They looked up. The next hopper was coming down from the sky. Sucus went to arrange the sand pile so the grabs could scoop up more. His feet in their canvas shoes were wet from the hosing. The hopper touched ground.

Bull! shouted Murat. Bull!

The cables slackened. The feed came out of the giant drum.

Murat took off his helmet and raised it above his head. A hundred metres above, Yannis nudged the cables so the hopper swung free of the nose of the drum and rose with its grey rain falling.

You should read history, said Murat.

The only book I read's a dictionary.

In history things often happen when nothing seems to be happening.

Like some nights.

Yes, history has nights and days, said Murat.

And now it's night?

Now it's night, it's been night for a long while.

Do you sleep? asked Sucus.

I'm impatient, and sometimes in the dark my impatience has a voice like an angel.

As he said this, Murat looked up at the clouds which in July often gathered in the late afternoon along the coastline like cattle coming in to drink.

What does she say, your angel?

She always says the same thing. If I am for myself, who are the others? she asks. If others are for themselves, who am I? If not now, when? If not here, where?

Where did she learn that?

They both looked up. Another hopper was coming down to be filled. When Yannis had hoisted it away, full, Sucus said:

Mine's no angel. Do you know what she says to me?

No.

Give me the earrings, she says. It's you who's given them to me and now I'll never take them off for anyone. Never.

. . .

Slowly the working day drew to its end. The last feed slid out of the giant drum and Sucus hosed its tongues so they should not be rough in the morning.

Yannis brought the crab home to his cabin and hoisted up the cables. One by one every engine on the site stopped. The very high clouds were turning green. Yannis slung his bag over his shoulder and came down to earth.

No doubt about it, my young friend, he said to Sucus in the hut where their lockers were, she was asking for a husband, your curly haired one.

What sort of papers do you need to be a crane driver? Sucus asked.

Papers! It's all here. Yannis thumped his chest.

No papers at all?

What you need is a head for geometry.

I know geometry, said Sucus.

You need eyes like a hawk.

I've got eyes like a falcon.

You need the concentration of an expresso, and a massive head for heights.

All right.

Go on, then. Shift up there and you'll find out. Climb!

Cato? Sucus was suddenly hesitant.

Cato's gone. You can fetch a postcard I forgot to bring down. I ought to post it. It's in the rack for plans, on the left of the throne. Go and try.

It's not locked?

We never lock up at home.

Sucus left the hut.

Don't look up or down, Yannis shouted after him, just look ahead. Three hundred and eight rungs. Count them if you want.

Crane, from the Greek *geranos*, meaning the bird with high legs. The higher Sucus climbed the invisible tower, the more pity he felt in his chest for his father who was dead. Two hundred and ninety-seven. Ten more.

At last he stepped onto the perforated platform, leant on the rail and, for the first time, looked down. On the ground it was dusk. Only the heap of polyester insulation panels showed up because they were white and slightly iridescent like the moon.

On the flat roof of the police station on Cauchy Street a man was running with a stick held up in the air. Suddenly, the man lunged forwards and struck the roof at his feet with the stick, then he knelt down to look closer at where he had struck. It took Sucus some time before he understood: the man was catching butterflies in a net.

The sky was full of a radiance, which was the colour of the inside of a cantaloupe melon, and the jib of the crane stretched out like a metal reef into a lake of light. The neons in the city below were switched on and the windows in many buildings shone like ice.

Sucus entered the cabin, found the postcard exactly where Yannis said it would be, and sat on the driver's throne. He read the address:

KYRIA XENIA IOANNIDE
ODOS ARTEMIDOS
KASTRO, SAMOS.

It was then he felt the crane swaying. Not in one direction but in two. Swaying on its feet like a man does after knocking back one glass of gnôle too many.

Now I'm alive, he told himself, now I can do anything!

crime

The creature whom the man in a track suit was trying to catch on the roof of the police station was a moth known as the Fiancée. She had brown fore wings the colour of bark, and yellow hind wings the colour of beaten eggs before you make an omelette. Her body was furry and sable coloured. About four centimetres in length, her favourite food is willow leaves. The man held the toe of the net in one hand and the wooden leg of the handle in the other. The Fiancée was flying very low and he came down on her from above. When she was well netted, he slipped in a pill box and she flew up into it because she thought she was flying towards the light. In a moment he would clap the lid on and bring the pill box out of the net.

The hunter was called Hector. When he smiled, his cheeks moved more than the corners of his mouth did. They moved upwards towards the lobes of his big ears. He was a heavy man. He made his way, smiling, past the transmitting aerial on the police station roof, to the door that gave onto the staircase.

The police station on Cauchy Street was nothing like the police station in the next village, where there are curtains in the windows, wives upstairs, and sometimes even the smell of cooking. Cauchy Street smelt of sweat and of slightly burnt glue—as if all the electrical equipment in the building were overheating. As for the sounds, they were of two kinds, depending upon the floor you got out at when the lift doors opened. On the ninth floor every sound was muffled. No sound carried. Everything was out of hearing. On other floors, because there were no carpets or curtains and the men wore boots and the doors were heavy and there were never any sleeping children, every sound was loud and every noise reverberated. Even a glass being filled with tap water sounded menacing. I have been on every floor.

In the toilet Hector took off his track suit and put on his dark blue uniform with gold epaulettes and a shirt with a buttoned-down collar. He was a Police Superintendent. He glanced into the mirror above the wash basin and adjusted his few strands of remaining hair. The thought of his retirement was troubling him, and every evening he tried to invent an excuse to stay late at the station. Off duty, he wandered around the offices, giving his opinion, asking questions, looking at old files. He was due to retire in three months. As Superintendent he allowed himself the eccentricity of wearing tennis shoes all day long. He pretended that at his age his feet suffered in leather. In truth, it was the silence of the tennis shoes that he liked. Now he walked stealthily down the corridor to his own room.

Behind his desk was a large cupboard of galvanised metal. He unlocked it. Such metal has no memory and is blind. From a pile of cassettes he selected one and, striding decisively across the floor, slid it into the VCR beneath the President's portrait. Switching off the light over his desk so that the room was almost dark, he settled back in his swivel chair to watch the tape. It began with a crowd of people on a metro platform. All the metro stations in Troy, like the banks, were under video surveillance. The people on the platform were waiting for a train. Up above in the streets it was winter, the men and women were wearing overcoats and gloves. Some were reading newspapers, others were jiggling their legs to earphone rhythms. Most were looking blankly across the tracks at other people who had left work and who were waiting for a train to take them home in the opposite direction. It was the same every evening.

Their faces were sad. They hadn't lost patience, but they'd lost heart. Perhaps heart comes back to them when they step out onto stations in distant suburbs and see the front windows of their houses, surrounded by trees, and lit up.

A little commotion begins. A man with a felt hat smashed onto the back of his head and a filthy overcoat too large for him goes to the edge of the platform. He has the determination of a man who believes too much in what he is doing. He is drunk. Under his arm he carries a carpet. Now he starts to point and shout at people. His gestures suggest he is insulting them. Yet his old man's words are lost for ever, for the video is soundless.

Those he addresses pretend not to hear. Two women, when

he pushes his way forward, walk away from him. He glances at them with a pained look and says something—as if now it is he who feels insulted. He rocks on his feet for consolation. Then he looks round for a distraction. He takes off his hat and waves at somebody, shouting again, this time with a smile. A man in a fur hat with a dispatch case looks up from his newspaper with disgust.

The Superintendent believed he was shouting a name—the name of the person he had just recognised on the opposite platform. During every viewing the Superintendent leant towards the video screen at this point, to try to lip-read the name. He believed it began with PON but he had never been able to decipher the last syllables.

There was a knock on the door. The Superintendent stopped the tape, switched on the light, leant back, placed his two hands on the armrests, and only then said:

Who is it?

Officer Albin reporting.

Come in.

The officer came in and saluted.

Well?

Washington Patrol have just picked up a runner.

Where is he?

In Reception.

How much did they find on him?

A hundred grammes.

Crack?

Crack, sir.

Is he talking?

No.

What name does he give?

Naisi.

Have we got tabs on him?

Not under that name.

Find out who he is and who feeds him.

Do you want to question him yourself, Superintendent?

Does he look cooperative?

Not yet.

Then I'll see him later. Pass him over to Sergeant Pasqua and keep me informed.

Officer Albin was about to salute and leave the room when Hector raised one finger of his right hand to retain him. The gesture was both deliberate and nonchalant—what mattered was that it was received as a command. Officer Albin stood there waiting. Hector reflected upon how, in a few months time, no act of his would ever again be acknowledged as a command, and this thought brought a pain to his chest. Each day, as the date of his retirement approached, he felt more lost. He studied the wedding ring on his second finger. Officer Albin still waited.

Tell Sergeant Pasqua I won't leave till he has something to tell me.

He flicked his finger almost invisibly, as a sign of dismissal.

Officer Albin saluted and turned. Hector listened to his footsteps receding along the stone corridor, then he extinguished the desk lamp and switched on the tape.

The people are still waiting for their train. A man wearing an overcoat with a black lamb's wool collar and, around his neck, a white silk scarf, places his attaché case on the platform and squats down beside it. He opens the case and then stands upright, holding a shining butcher's axe. His movements are decisive and calm. He jumps onto the tracks, crosses them, and leaps like an athlete up onto the platform beside the drunk old man with the carpet under his arm. The old man screws up his face like a baby. The man with the axe fells him with one terrible blow delivered to the back of the neck. The victim crumples and falls to the ground.

The assassin crosses the tracks again, puts the dripping weapon back in his attaché case, and walks slowly towards the exit at the end of the platform. The crowd separates to let him through.

No one makes a move or kneels down to help the old man. He lies sprawled on the platform in an empty circle. A train draws in. Then a second train. Their doors open. Passengers get on and off. The trains leave. On the deserted platform the corpse lies there, in its dark stain.

The victim's name was Gilbert d'Ormesson. On the day following his murder, the police computer located his dossier in less than two minutes. D'Ormesson; born in Constantine, November 5, 1919; several arrests for drunken and disorderly behaviour; no fixed address; decorated with the Military Medal, 1945.

In the wallet found in his overcoat there was a photograph of a woman who looked like a cabaret artist, 1960s style. Clipped to this photo were three others of a black miniature poodle. On the back of one was written: Gilly, my love. After his death, no relative or acquaintance came forward.

Six months passed. Despite the hundreds of witnesses, the man with the butcher's chopper was not identified. Hector toyed with the idea that the old man might have been involved in small-time blackmail. Yet when he listened to his lifelong experience, he knew now that the metro murder would soon join the great majority of crimes: those which are unsolved.

Last night, down the road to the village, the frogs were returning to our lake by the rocks. Hundreds of thousands of them hopping towards the thawed green water. They converge on the lake from all sides, when the moon is waxing. In their haste to begin, the females hop with the males on their backs. Then they jump into the water together, and the couple stay attached for days, until the female lays her eggs, which the male, still on her back, still clutching her, fertilises as they drop into the water. They do this every year, unless there is a danger of their being too many. When this happens they stop mating. People wonder how frogs know. On summer nights in the lake they croak for hours on end, and the strength of their chorus tells them how many they are. When their croaking is too loud, they become chaste for a season.

If the Superintendent asked me, I could also explain to him the metro murder. One morning, the killer placed a brand-new butcher's chopper in his attaché case because he hoped to kill somebody. He did not yet know who. When he left home and kissed his wife goodbye, the extra weight in his attaché case upheld him. He walked jauntily to the station. It was not the first time he had left home with a chopper. In fact it was the seventh or eighth. He wanted to kill so his name would mean something for ever, so God would notice him. But he was not a man who could kill indiscriminately. On the other days, when he'd found no one to kill, he did his usual work in the office—he worked for an insurance company; he went to his usual café for lunch, and in the evening he came home on his usual train, as if carrying a butcher's chopper wrapped in black satin in his attaché case was the most usual thing in the world. The black satin he'd found in his wife's wardrobe. She had bought it eight years before to make into a nightdress, yet since their two children were born, she had given up making clothes for herself. The day he saw the old drunk on the metro platform, his heart leapt with joy. His victim was there, he told himself. He knelt down on the platform to listen for a train. No, there was no train. This was the sign that God was willing. So he flew across the tracks. After he had killed the old man, he felt agreeably weak. As he climbed up from the lines onto the platform, he promised himself that he would take a taxi home. Which is what he did.

In the Interrogation Unit on the ninth floor, Sergeant Pasqua went to the sink and opened a can of beer. Naisi was seated on a bench against a wall, his arms behind his back, wrists handcuffed. He could feel the clots of blood with his tongue, like bleeding gooseberries. Yet he did not dare spit them out. If he spat, he'd be hit again.

Tell us, you fucker!

Tell you what?

You know, fucker.

Your football team won last week, didn't they, Sarge?

Start telling.

What?

Who supplies?

I heard they played well.

Who gives you the news?

Hoo does.

Don't get fresh with me, fucker.

Hoo pays too, and Hoo collects.

What's his name?

Told you, Sergeant, Hoo. Chinese.

You got more? said the sergeant, throwing away the can of beer. Naisi knew that whatever he replied would not be heard. But he could not prevent one of the gooseberries dripping from the corner of his mouth.

Start telling.

When a man is handcuffed, he becomes like a bird who can't fly. Crippled, he can only scurry like a mouse. Striking a prisoner who is handcuffed produces new words, new cries.

Ble!

Who do you get it from?

Ble!

I'll make you nobody.

On my own.

Take that, bastard. Shit is. Shit is. Shit is what you deserve.

Pasqua knocked Naisi onto the floor and dragged him over to the toilet. I have known all kinds of violent men. There is no violence, however terrible, that I have not seen. Yet usually they were as helpless as their victims. Sergeant Pasqua was different. His violence was as routine as a dog scratching behind its ears.

Shit is. Shit is what you're going to eat. Start telling.

Blu!

Who do you get it from?

Dug.

Dog what?

Dug.

Address?

Ble.

Pasqua kicked the prisoner in the stomach.

Start telling.

Morio.

Address?

Twenty-one twenty-five Tortoise Hill.

What's Morio for a name?

It's what he uses.

Where do you meet him?

City Aquarium, by the turtles.

Okay. If you're lying, the next time you're brought in here, you get them pulped, see? Pulped—no more fucky-fucky.

. . .

Hector arrived on the ninth floor by lift. He had put on his outdoor shoes and dark glasses. The shoes because he intended to go home afterwards without returning to his office, the glasses because he always wore them when he visited the Interrogation Unit. They prevented any appeal to the eyes.

The Superintendent opened the door and saw a man wearing calf-coloured boots with golden buckles smoking a cigarette. The man was no longer handcuffed. There was blood on his face but no signs of collapse. The Superintendent considered himself an expert in reading such signs, which often begin at the corner of the mouth or in the way fingers are held.

Where did it come from? he asked the prisoner.

Probably from Colombia, replied Naisi.

Everything comes from Colombia, doesn't it?

Now you're talking, Super.

Who handled it before you did?

One of your men here in the station.

At this point Sergeant Pasqua allowed each of his hundred kilos to give weight to the four words he now pronounced:

He has grassed, sir.

So, he's grassed, has he? Like a heifer he's grassed, you say, Sergeant!

Like a rhino, said Naisi, not a heifer.

What's he given you, Sergeant?

The name of Morio.

Morio, Morio? Operating where?

Twenty-one twenty-five Tortoise Hill.

Brilliant, Sergeant. I think I should see to it that your rota gets changed.

Routine, sir.

Brilliant, Sergeant.

Thank you, sir.

Perhaps you've spent a little too much time up here. A few months at ground level might do you a world of good, Pasqua. Have you tried tracking down somebody on Tortoise Hill?

Never, sir. Tortoise Hill is recent, sir.

You can find nothing and nobody there. It's worse than Rat. It's worse that Tepito. They've got Uzis there. He's made you a present of nothing.

He won't do it a second time. Give me half an hour.

Like a rhino, Superintendent. I told you I grassed like a rhino, said Naisi.

Was the stuff planted on him? demanded Hector.

He's had his hands on plenty, trust my nose, Superintendent.

Was it planted?

Let's say it was found, Superintendent, a few minutes after they frisked me, said Naisi.

Turn him out.

Give me—

I've told you, Sergeant. Turn him out.

. . .

As the Superintendent passed through Reception, the two police officers on duty wished him good-night. Under his breath one of them muttered: Geriatric Ward! Then the two of them went on looking at the comic they had hidden under the counter.

In the story they were reading, a chauffeur was driving a large limousine. In the back of the car were David and George and a woman called Antoinette. She had her legs apart. Antoinette, you're still full of spunk, said David. Of course, she replied, you came everywhere! Ah, Antoinette, said George. Why don't you begin again? she suggested. You've knocked us both out, said David. Then I'll have to find out what the chauffeur is made of, said the insatiable Antoinette. She leant forward and put her tongue in the chauffeur's ear . . . The two police officers turned the page and read on, both imagining they were the chauffeur.

When he first left the village, age fourteen, Hector wept. I saw him wiping his eyes with his sleeve outside the door of the Republican Lyre. Then he ran down the steps to get into the bus and he shouted to his friends: You'd better lock up all your chicks and chickens when I get back!

He only came back twice.

Peasants make solid policemen, for they have the necessary energy, obstinacy, and toughness. But power isn't the same thing as earth, and, as policemen, they seldom become wise. After a number of years in the city, Hector married Susanna, the daughter of a disgraced army officer. She had auburn hair, a milky, delicate skin, and a profile like they engrave on coins. The first time he saw her she was wearing golden sandals. It was Hector's assurance that attracted Susanna. He was capable and daring. He was not, like her father, ridden with doubt. Even his bragging she considered as a kind of froth bubbling around his capabilities. She told her friends there was nothing Hector couldn't handle, and she nicknamed him Ram, the *bélier*. With her help he would become Chief Constable. And one day he would take her away, she dreamed, from sprawling Troy to a nobler city such as Tenochtitlan, where nobody would have to handle anything except chalices and anointing oils and flowers, flowers . . .

You're home later than ever, she said to him.

Policemen aren't librarians.

That's new. Usually you say policemen aren't train drivers.

Same thing.

And in a few months' time, Hector, you won't be a policeman.

Like you say, my dear, I won't be a policeman.

It was suffocating this afternoon, I felt so weak I didn't go to my gym class.

Why didn't you put the fan on?

Fan! All our friends have air conditioning, they've had air conditioning for years, but not us, not poor us, because Hector couldn't make it higher than a Superintendent, his resources were exhausted. He's spent himself. He's reached his limit, hasn't he?

I'd say you've been drinking again, Susanna.

I most certainly have not—

The evidence suggests—

The evidence suggests . . . You're not in the station any more. You're at home. You've come home. And the one person in the world you can't question, Hector, is me. And you can't question me because I'm your own failure.

Pour me a coffee.

Then take off your gun.

With ice.

And your sun glasses. It was a great mistake, Hector, when you stopped drinking, you never relax now.

You know why I did.

To set me an example! But we had our laughs. It's a good two years since I've seen you laugh.

Not many jokes come my way, Susanna.

I'll tell you a joke.

Later.

Of course! Wait till he orders his joke! Then place it on a tray and serve it with salted almonds. How do you like your joke cooked, sir? Crude, medium, or well-done?

Susanna, I've had a hard day and I'd like to eat. Perhaps it would be good for you to eat too.

The Superintendent would like to eat what his wife has spent the afternoon preparing. Well, his wife has prepared a very special menu tonight. She's prepared a joke with a shallot sauce!

Shh!

Shallot sauce, yes.

Don't drink any more now, Susanna.

He let himself out of the French window and walked across the lawn. In the house next door lived a young couple who were both dentists. Soon they would make enough money to move on to a bigger house and garden. How am I going to end my days here? he asked himself for the thousandth time. And for the thousandth time he heard a child's voice say: I'd rather die.

The last time he had tried to persuade Susanna that when he retired they should build a house in his village, on the land he had inherited from his aunt above the Republican Lyre, Susanna had finished her glass, put her swanlike arms round his neck, and said: You must be out of your mind, darling, I've told you a hundred times I'm not going to end my days living with a nag-who-has-a-broken-leg! That's how the *bled* is called, isn't it?

Now he walked across the lawn towards two flowering azalea bushes. It came to him that the common names of moths and butterflies resembled some of the nicknames given to criminals and their companions: the Fiancée, Robert the Demon, the Big Tortoise, Morio, the Mourning Suit, Blue Eyes.

From where he stood between the azaleas, his head full of names, he could distinguish the sea he wanted to cross and the arc lights of the docks.

Ram, she called, come and listen to my joke . . .

sky

S ucus woke up early. Every morning the living room
smelt of ironing. He could see two piles of ironed table cloths
and napkins on the table. They were pale green and they
came from a restaurant at the fashionable end of Cachan
called Las Vegas. In the middle of each table cloth, when it
was unfolded, there was printed a silhouette, wine red, of a
dancer walking on tip-toe. Since Branch's death, his mother
took in ironing.

A southwest wind off the sea was blowing rain against the
living room window on the fourteenth floor. The walls of the
room were still covered with scarves to hide the damp stains.
A chink of light appeared under the bedroom door. Behind
it Wislawa was putting on her dressing gown, which, since
her husband's death, had become too big for her.

For men it is different, they don't have the same habit of following as women do. Men mourn, of course. Marcel, who kidnapped the inspectors, placed flowers on the table by the empty side of his wedding bed every night after Nicole died. Men feel left behind, abandoned. Women grieve more than mourn, and they grieve for what has happened to their dead. This is why they follow them through the underworld.

Each morning when she came into the living room, Wislawa had the look of a widow who had been travelling throughout the night.

Here's a clean pair of underpants and a vest for you, she said.

It's raining, said Sucus.

It's bound to rain from time to time.

It was raining yesterday too.

I'll make the coffee. You get out of bed. You'd do well to take your oilskins today.

Can't work in them. Are my shoes dry?

Wear your gum boots.

They fill up with water.

Then empty them from time to time.

From time to time! From time to time! You've no idea what it's like on a building site. You've never worked on one, so you don't know.

Your father did.

He didn't.

Clement did every job under the sun.

He told me he opened oysters for forty years and nothing else.

At least your poor father has one worry less, now you're earning.

Doesn't he have better things to think about where he's gone?

Not yet, not yet, it's too soon.

You're going to make the coffee?

Not till you're out of bed.

Please!

If you work well, you could be a foreman one day.

A foreman! God forbid. You should see Cato . . . A crane driver, yes. But, you need a certificate of some sort.

You could go to evening classes and work for the certificate.

In the evening, mother, I've got better things to do. Did Zsuzsa come round yesterday?

Out of bed! No, she didn't.

What have you got against her? She brought you some fish and she cooked them.

She cooks well.

So then?

Nothing. Get out of bed.

She cooks well, so?

Clement should be here to see you like this! You'll be late for work.

.   .   .

All over Troy, the rain of the summer's end was pouring down rooves: rooves of tile, concrete, slate, corrugated iron, tarpaulin, wood, schist, cardboard, glass, old sacking, cement, polyester. From some it ran off into shining galvanised gutters, into others it soaked, and some it destroyed. West of Cachan, in the direction of Swansea, in the district of San Isidro, Yannis lived on the third floor of an apartment block.

On the same wet morning, his mother came out of her bedroom in a dressing gown borrowed from Sonia, her daughter-in-law, which was too skimpy for her. At home, on the island, she put on a dress, not a dressing gown, as soon as she got out of bed. She had a face so weathered by the sea and the sun that she almost looked as if she had been smoked like a ham or a fish. But her eyes, despite her age, were clear and blue. Whatever she was doing—putting up her long white hair into a chignon, pouring hot water onto coffee, washing clothes, making tarama—she did with such assurance that it was impossible to help her, or even be beside her.

At first she had been delighted to see her granddaughters and had been reduced to silence by the sight of so many new things and people. Then, after about a week, she had started to make her comments. First she spoke to her daughter-in-law when the two women found themselves alone, after the girls had gone off to school. But when it became clear to her that Sonia only understood a few words of Greek—she was an Armenian—and, furthermore, pretended to be deaf, she muttered to herself for hours and became singleminded about seizing every opportunity of talking to her son whenever she could corner him. This was why she got up at half past five in the morning to make his coffee before he went to work.

You have a good job, Yannis, she said, you earn good money and you deserve it. There were five beautiful women on Samos who would have packed and arranged and unpacked their doweries every night, so eager would they have been to marry you, if you gave the word, you who work up there alone in the sky like a heavenly fisherman. So you married a foreigner here in the city and your daughters don't speak Greek and your wife has not yet given you a son and you earn good money, this is what I want to tell you, but you do not husband it, you let it be wasted, the good money you earn in the sky, this money is spent on the first whim that enters her head. She spends as if she had no faith in the future, she's bird-witted. Look in the bathroom, Yannis, I did not know there were so many different lotions on this earth for women.

Some are for me, said her son.

The Siren sisters did not have more and they lured men to their death. Open the wardrobe in the children's room and it is like, it is like switching on a television set! Nothing, nothing in it will last, there's not a rag there for your grand-children, it is trash. Why are there cockroaches in your home? I will tell you, my son. They have come because there is no husbandry here, cockroaches are a sign of heedlessness.

I tell you every morning, Mother, we are not on Samos here. The cockroaches are in the whole building.

It's Babylon!

We live here. I invited you here so you could see how we live.

The house is waiting for you, Yannis, it will always be waiting for you.

We've made a life here in the city.

Everyone grows old, my boy. And with age everyone's eye-sight fails a little. I don't need to see more than I do in order to know. I know because I feel. You work in the sky like a god, and you are lost!

You see nothing!

Why do you shout at me?

I have to go now.

Have a good day, my son.

Yannis drove to the building site on Park Avenue. He had a small Renault. Already the streets were full, the cars fender to fender. It was raining in torrents and through the windshield the lights were tangled like yellow wool. Yannis, the crane driver, was thinking about his women . . .

It's not Sonia's fault if she's a little scatterbrained. It's not Mother's fault if she's never left Samos. But why can't they leave me in peace? He was driving less smoothly than usual. Suddenly, he had to slam on his brakes to avoid a woman pushing a grown-up figure across the street in a gigantic pram. He frowned. The pram made him think of babies. After a month with four women in the flat, he would like to have a son . . . he would call him Alexander.

Underneath the rubber sheet of the pram the woman was pushing, sat a man, huddled up, his hands on his lap, his head lolling a little. The woman stopped on the pavement and adjusted the hat on the man's head so that it sheltered him better from the rain. You mustn't get cold, she said, if you catch cold I'll have no end of trouble with you. I know you—when your nose is running, you stop eating, you refuse to eat, and your tummy goes hard. Let me tuck your foot under the sheet, they're not waterproof these boots and you'll get soaked. We don't have to cross the road again, my love, till we get to Park Avenue. You like passing by there, don't you? You like watching the big cranes.

. . .

On the building site all the men had taken shelter in the locker room. When Yannis arrived the goddess man was telling a joke. Sucus was reading in a newspaper a story about dolphins being trained to protect nuclear submarines.

Cato flung open the door and stared at the men leaning against the walls.

What are you waiting for, you lazy buggers? Out! Get out on the job.

Murat took a step forward and bowed very slightly, as if about to award a public prize.

Can I say something, Mr. Cato? I would suggest we wait until it's raining a little less.

Is that what you would suggest! Jesus!

Under these weather conditions, Mr. Cato, the safety of the workers on the site is at risk.

You talk like a fucking lawyer. You get your foreign mouth around big words! You'd better watch it or I'll have you blacked. No work anywhere. See? Out! Get out there now!

Not a single builder moved.

It's a mud swamp out there, Mr. Cato.

Mud or shit, it's the same to me. We're eight days behind schedule.

Men'll be sliding in all directions. Quite apart from the hazard to health working all day in drenched clothes.

Hazard to health my arse! This isn't a nursery school. Any man who needs a cape can go and get one from stores. I want the six casings set up yesterday poured. See? Now out!

Still nobody moved. Cato approached Murat with his fists up.

Drop your knife! Cato hissed.

I'm not moving, said the Turk.

Then you're fired. Out, the rest of you! Are you deaf or what? I said outside. You want to be fired, the lot of you? Shit! What's the matter with you?

The twenty men in the wooden hut, big-handed and sullen,

refused to move. The air was muggy with their breath and damp clothes. No one spoke. The floor boards creaked under their heavy boots. They filled the little hut the way a single elephant would fill a railway wagon. Eventually the goddess man said: You put Murat back on the payroll or none of us work today.

Cato turned away to look out the window. He stuck his hands in his belt. The elephant shifted its weight. Finally Cato spoke:

Look, it's raining less already. Get out there, the lot of you, Murat included! We've had our little yap, now get to work.

It was true that the falling rain was less heavy. Three builders moved towards the door. The others followed. Some of the men tied plastic sacks over their heads. Murat was the last to leave.

. . .

The first hopper was there to be filled. When Murat waved, Yannis hoisted a little clumsily and the load swung sideways on its cables so that grey cement slurped over to fall with the small rain onto the muddy earth.

The wind was coming in squalls. In the cabin Yannis glanced at the wind gauge to see whether the gusts were exceeding the statutory fifty kilometres per hour. Not yet. The rhythm of the long wiper blades as they swept backwards and forwards across the glass wall of the cabin reminded him of two oars from long ago, when his father used to row a boat. He must have been no more than six, for by the time he was seven his father had drowned. Another squall hit the crane like a wave.

On the ground, the sudden gusts whipped the men's wet

clothes against their bodies, and those who were able ducked their heads behind their shoulders to shelter their faces against the rain. Sucus was shifting sand towards the crabs of the cement mixer. The sand was twice as heavy as usual. With his feet wet and water trickling down his neck and his right shovelling shoulder a little stiff, he thought of Zsuzsa. He thought, as men have always done under rough conditions, of her warmth and softness, of how she was the opposite of shifting wet sand in squalls of rain.

The first time he'd seen her without a stitch of clothing on, the first time he'd seen her hidden hair, darker than he had imagined in any dream, he thought he was the luckiest man on earth. She was standing there before him and she was making everything else until the end fade into nothingness!

Bull! shouted Murat as the hopper came down.

The mixer spewed out its liquid concrete. Murat threw the switch and the feeding stopped, the drum rotating in the opposite direction, tongue lolling. Sucus, leaning on his shovel, watched.

It was then Murat noticed that one of the lifting chains looked out of place. He hesitated. They had just put in two tons of concrete. If two tons of concrete fell out of the sky as the crane took the load off . . . From where he was on the ground he couldn't properly see the rings the chains were threaded through. He found a foothold and pulled himself up the hopper to look more closely.

Another squall hit the crane, seriously reducing visibility. The air became like sea. Yannis thought he saw Murat wave his helmet in the air. He pressed the appropriate black button.

The hopper started its ascension into the sky with Murat still clinging to it.

No! he shouted. Bull! Bull! The wind blew his words away. Only Sucus heard them and saw what was happening.

Let go! Let go! yelled Sucus.

It would have been simple for Murat to jump during these first few seconds, but there are situations in which the will to survive issues mad orders and a paralysis sets in. Once I saw a dog on river ice which was breaking up. The dog was standing on a slab that had broken loose and was carrying him downstream. It couldn't decide whether to jump or stay put. Its forelegs wanted to do one thing, its hind legs the opposite. In the same way Murat's hands refused to loosen their grip, as the hopper rose into the air above the cement mixer.

Frantic, Sucus scrambled up the mud bank so as to be directly under the hopper. There he fell onto his knees and looked up at the great ladle already four metres off the ground, and about to disappear into the sky. Murat was hanging by his arms, legs dangling. Jump! Murat! Jump! Sucus prayed and implored. The words carried. Murat heard them and this time, miraculously, his hands obeyed. They let go and he fell five metres down on to the earth, just beside Sucus.

Murat!

The Turk was face to the ground. For what seemed a year he didn't stir. At last, he turned his head.

Newborn, don't fret, he said, I think one of my legs is broken. It's better I don't move.

The squall had passed. There appeared the first brief sunshine of the day. Yet both men on the ground were shivering.

Yannis, in his cabin, realised that something unusual had occurred on the ground below. Why was the Turk lying face down in the mud? What was the young man who wanted to be a crane driver doing on his knees beside him? He hauled up and swung the jib to the west. Cato was running towards the cement plant waving his arms. The young man had gotten to his feet and was walking towards Cato. Both of them stopped abruptly, facing one another. Then the young man hit the foreman in the face and the foreman, taken by surprise, stepped backwards, slipped and fell. Now the young man returned to the Turk, who hadn't moved and was still lying spread-eagled on the yellow mud. It was at this moment that Yannis became convinced there had been an accident.

He had to deliver the hopper to the pouring or the concrete would set. When this was done, he stopped the crane and came out of the cabin. Arching over the city towards the east there was a rainbow. He began to descend the ladder much more slowly than usual. His silhouette against the sky, as he descended, showed a man weighed down by doubt.

Sucus did not really decide in which direction to walk: he just walked. The rain had lessened to a slight drizzle. When taxis pulled up at the Metropole Hotel the hall porters no longer held scarlet umbrellas aloft. In the sky above the building site both cranes were working again, jibs turning. Cato had sacked Sucus on the spot. Murat had been taken away on a stretcher.

Sucus strode down Park Avenue towards Carouge. It was an area full of banks. The banks clustered together, discouraging any building where money might be exchanged for pleasure. In the banks nothing was hidden except money, every pore of these buildings was under surveillance, every one of their surfaces polished as if shaved for an operation. This was why to steal from them was almost as much a challenge as walking on the moon, and the popular heroes in the city were men like Nestor, or Margarlon, or Diomedes, robbers whose hauls had become legendary. As he passed the lunar banks, Sucus grasped the reindeer knife on his belt.

After ten minutes he came to Gentilly, the district of the cloth merchants, with shops, warehouses, wholesalers, and factories. In the narrow streets buyers, sellers, messengers, brokers, tea boys, jostled each other all day. Porters carried piles of garments as high as themselves, bound with string, garments women had finished at home now being returned to their contractors. Everybody Sucus passed or knocked against was busy on a small errand, urgent for somebody somewhere.

The last clouds had been blown away. The buildings on the distant hills looked white in the sunlight. The fishmongers sprinkled more broken ice on their fish, and Sucus on the jostling sidewalk remembered how his father had told him about a shepherd in the alpage. He didn't remember the man's name. All he recalled was that the man said something and the air was so still, the man so alone, that the mountain echoed his voice.

As if the sound came from the mountains, a cock crowed. Sucus stopped and looked round. An old woman, toothless, with a nose like a beak, was sitting on an upturned wooden box in a doorway. Between her legs was a basket holding several white chickens. Realising she had stopped in his tracks the young man covered in cement dust, the old woman crowed again and beckoned to him.

A plump young white chicken, she called, three thousand nine hundred!

For that price! . . . And Sucus laughed the bargaining laugh.

Come over here and I'll tell you a story.

Sucus approached.

It happened to my neighbour. She and I live beyond the

oil tanks, where the fields start. She has a husband, this neighbour, a husband who likes the booze. On Saturday evening he asks some of his cronies home and they start drinking in the kitchen, drinking and singing. His wife says she's going to bed. A little later the husband falls asleep in his chair. Are you listening to me, boy? Or are you looking at the white chickens? I'm too blind to see. Listen. One of the husband's cronies had an idea: Let's play a joke on him, he said. It's Easter, he said, they're bound to have a chicken, look in the ice box. Sure enough, they found one. Cut off its head and give me the neck, said the joker. Okay. Now open his fly and let the little neck hang out as it should! That's what the old men did in the kitchen. Then they went home. At about five in the morning the wife wakes up in her big bed, she can't hear any voices, and her husband isn't beside her. So she gets up. She opens the kitchen door, and what does she see? Do you know what she saw? She saw the cat eating her hubby's zizi! . . .

I'll give it to you, young man, because you laughed so much, for twenty-five hundred!

Sucus carried the live white chicken upside down by its legs along the Shepherd's Bush Road. It was the chicken he was holding that told him where to go.

He passed a woman pushing a pram with a grown-up man in it. He stopped to watch. The woman bent down to speak to the man in the pram.

Are you too hot, my love? I don't want you sweating, it always puts you in a bad mood. Is the sun in your eyes? We've got to get to Lions so we can pick up the music sheets, otherwise I won't have enough. Bend your knee now. Be good and bend your knee. Then I can pull up your trouser bottom, my love. We have a lot of music to write . . .

The paths up Rat Hill were muddy and Sucus slipped several times. Once he fell on the chicken who started to cackle very loud, hoping that all the cocks in the world would come to her aid. Outside the Blue House there was nobody, but the door was open. Inside, Naisi was sitting on a chair by the window, wiping with an oily cloth a Zig submachine gun which lay across his knees.

What did you do, Brother-in-Law?

I hit the boss.

You shouldn't have done that, he said.

It happened before I could stop it.

Never hit the boss unless you kill him. He can always hit harder. Besides, it's too intimate.

I knocked him down.

And you got sacked, no? He got up off the ground and you got put down in the shit, no? You can read, I suppose?

Sucus nodded.

Zsuzsa can't read.

And you, asked Sucus, you read?

Me? I'm the first reading member of the family. They kept me four years in their zaouia. They taught me how to read and they taught me about God. You can't fiddle with him. That's what I learnt about God . . . in one sentence. It was in this zaouia I first touched a piano. The piano was in a cellar where they made yoghurt, and the cook, he was black, he taught me the notes. He loved to play a number of his own called "Your Balls Are Hanging Out." To this day I can't play it without smelling damp cloth and heated milk. Then I got pregnant.

You're joking.

I got found with Indian hemp.

Naisi smiled a smile as enigmatic as the Buddha's. It was

hard to know whether it was a smile of regret, of humor, or of courage before the worst possible news.

This is what I wanted to show you.

Naisi handed a folded newspaper to Sucus, who read the small headline: TORTOISE HILL DEFIES INTERPOL. ESCAPE NETWORK UNFOLLOWABLE SAYS IDENTITY MAN.

Whatever happens, Brother-in-Law, don't forget, Zsuzsa can't read.

Meaning what?

Always give her a second chance.

Naisi got up, opened his mother's wardrobe, and placed the gun carefully on the top shelf behind the shoes.

What applies to them doesn't apply to us, Brother-in-Law. Never forget it, otherwise you'll get hurt.

He turned round from the wardrobe to face Sucus. A golden mask covered his face. The expression of the mask was sad, as if no other colour in the world was more used, more fatigued than gold. Through the slits Sucus could see the same lost blue eyes.

I wear it some nights when I play at the Alhambra, Naisi explained, without taking it off.

He sat down, sprawling, on the one chair. They look the same in the morgue as we do, Naisi said, they have the same blood groups as we do. But we and they have nothing in common.

My father said the same thing.

Did he?

He said there were peasants and there were those who fed off the peasants.

Peasants! I'm talking about the twenty-first century, I'm talking about today and tomorrow.

Sucus was still holding the chicken.

We're born outside the law and whatever we do, we break it, said Naisi. They're born inside and whatever they do, they're protected. If you need to hit without killing, hit those who love you, not them. What applies to them doesn't apply to us. Take apples. They eat an apple for their health. We eat an apple because one of us stole it. Take cars. They drive because they've got a rendezvous. We drive to get away. Building a house! They build to invest their money and leave it to their children. We build to have a roof. Fucking! They fuck to get kicks! Naisi took off the mask and dropped it onto the floor. I fuck to die! And you?

Sucus knew before he turned round that Zsuzsa was standing behind him.

Your man just punched the foreman, said Naisi.

What the hell made him do that?

I didn't think. I just hit.

Give her to me, said Zsuzsa.

She turned the chicken the right way up so it sat on her hand, against her breast.

It's when they've abandoned all hope that chickens become calm. She stroked its back.

Cato deserved it, said Sucus.

Ah, my silky one, murmured Zsuzsa, rubbing her chin over the white wing feathers.

I got the sack, said Sucus. For my mother it's going to be . . .

I know.

It was stupid. For my mother it—

Don't worry, Flag. I'll tell you what we're going to do. We'll go into town. We'll go and say goodbye to your fucking building site. And we'll go and see your mother. Wait five minutes.

She slipped out, the chicken under her arm. The two men heard the last soft cluck being drawn from its throat.

The neighbours all bring their poultry for her to kill, said Naisi, she's done it since she was ten. She never frightens them.

Must be the way she holds them, said Sucus.

When we were kids, not here but beyond Swansea, before they cleared us off with their bulldozers, we had a goat and it was always Zsuzsa who milked it. She learnt to milk goats before she learnt to count.

. . .

I'm going to disappear, said Zsuzsa, on their way down to the city.

She put herself behind Sucus and pressed her body hard against his.

Walk! she ordered.

She moved each of her legs with his, and clung very close to him. Anyone approaching would have seen the silhouette of a single figure.

She's gone! she whispered.

Sucus was burning with desire.

As an old woman, I know. Burning is the word. His zizi felt as if it would spurt blood if it weren't cooled. And his blood felt as if it were boiling. This was happening inside his body. Outside his body it was worse. At his age, time is very long and it's length breeds a terrible impatience. He felt he would be swallowed up by time if he didn't have her now.

Where can we go? he muttered over his shoulder.
Go on walking, big one, she's gone!

Zsuzsa's desire was different from his. Nothing threatened
to swallow her up. She didn't have to cross any open space
to arrive where she wanted to be with Sucus. She didn't have
to leave her forest. The forest was her nature. She wandered
about in it, she lay down in it, she looked up from it into the
sky. She knew the calls of many of its animals, but not all.
And she believed Sucus was in the forest. All she had to do
was to find where he was hiding. He was never in the same
spot. And he was never far. What she wanted most to do was
to uncover him and cover him and uncover him again. Most
berries are hidden by leaves, some are protected by thorns.
Her desire was to find in her forest, close to the ground, the
cluster of Sucus. Since she never had to leave the forest, it
didn't matter how long it took.

By now they were in Carouge, where Sucus had been that
morning. It was getting dark. A jetliner, wing lights flashing,
was crossing the sky.
I'll tell you what I saw today, Flag, you won't believe me!
It was black and very low on the ground and it looked like
an electric razor. Inside it was red leather. The steering wheel
was white snake skin. Had a CD player and a special sound

system. Easy to get out—I had a good look—four screws and only one flange to cut.

A Cormorant?

No, the hood wasn't long enough. But listen—

I'm listening.

It's there, parked in the street. Behind Budapest Station. Around Sankt Pauli. Along comes Mr. Director. He has bad teeth, I can tell you. The colour of mutton fat. In his pocket he's got a zapper. He zaps and a light by each car door goes on. He zaps again: the four doors unlock and open a couple of inches. He's still standing there in the building doorway. Zap! The doors shut. Zap! The engine starts. Zap. It backs up, and it's ready to go! Beep beep! Mr. Director gets in and drives off! One day, Flag, we're going to have a car like that!

Did you get his number?

No. But I got his zapper!

She threw what looked like a tiny pocket calculator into the air and caught it with both hands.

Let me see!

Not now, Flag, and she started laughing.

I know where we'll go, said Sucus.

They were on the sidewalk beside the tall wooden fence that screened off the Mond Bank building site. Following the fence, he lead her off Park Avenue and down a side street.

One day I'll buy you a car with a zapper, she said.

They came to a small locked door in the fence. Just past the door he pushed a plank sideways. Then another.

We came through here every day to get beer from the vending machine in the metro.

Once inside, he carefully placed the planks back against the fence.

At night, half finished, the building looked like the ruin

from Roman times which was in our village schoolbook. The same black holes where the doors and windows should be, the same uneven skyline, the same scale, as if it were the plaything of a giant for whom the sky was no bigger than a pillow.

We're going up there! he said.

Up where, Flag?

The crane there.

Which one?

The father.

Father?

The tall one.

It's so high, Flag.

There's a ladder.

I can't see it.

There's a cabin.

It'll be locked, Flag.

We never lock up at home. Quick. Before we're spotted.

He took her hand and lead her to the foot of the crane.

There are three hundred and eight rungs, he said, you can count them if you like. Don't look up and don't look down. Just count.

You go first, she said, I'll follow.

They started climbing.

Below them were a myriad of lights. For each light there were at least ten people, each one with a name. These people were climbing stairs, crossing streets, sleeping, working, talking, touching one another, suffering, dying, eating, drinking themselves to death, making music, vomiting, planning, going under, surviving. Their numbers multiplied every week. And the weight of the deaths that occurred in Troy never suppressed the lightness of the births.

We're here, said Sucus, look down.
Don't break my fingers, said Zsuzsa.
It's open.
Are you sure it's open?
Take off your dress, Zsuzsa.

It seems to me Zsuzsa and Sucus were making love when the story began.

I've never been so tall, said Zsuzsa.
Can you feel it? Can you feel it swaying?
No one will ever make me as tall as this.
One day you'll fly in a plane!
It'll never go as high as we are now.
A Boeing 747 to Paris!
No, Flag, nobody in my life will bring me as high as you've done tonight.

marriage

On the right of the stove in my kitchen, there's a little lever to operate a damper which increases or reduces the draught of air being sucked up into the chimney pipe. The mechanism is simple enough for an old woman to understand. Pushing the lever up or down turns a bar which is attached to a circle of thin metal which has the same dimensions as the pipe. When it's upright it shuts off, and when it's horizontal it lets the air go up. Last year, the buff broke off the bar and the fire roared all the time, so I went to César, the blacksmith, and asked him if he could repair it. It was an insult to ask him this, like asking a cobbler to sew on a button. But he looked at me and said, as if we were both fifty years younger: Since it's for you, I'll mend it! Two days later I passed by and there was the damper, repaired and waiting for me. César wasn't at home, so I took it and left for him on his workbench a pot of my honey. Several months later he died. Now every time I move the lever up or down, I think of César, the dead blacksmith, and I thank him as I hear the breath in the chimney becoming weaker or stronger. César, I whisper, you are in my fire!

It was getting dark in Troy. Sucus was sprawled on his bed reading about a marriage between a famous millionaire and an Australian film star. The millionaire was reported to have said: This is my fifth and last marriage, for I'm old enough today to know what I want. He was sixty-two, the bride twenty-three. Sucus dropped his newspaper onto the floor beside the bed.

Do you remember the last time you went to the village, Maman?

Wislawa put down her iron and looked through the fourteenth-storey window as if she could see—not the lead ingots of other Trojan buildings, but a mountain.

The last time I was in the village, Sucus, I was pregnant with you.

Was it snowing?

She laughed. No, it was summer, the time of the haymaking. They wouldn't let me fork up the hay. They said it was too risky with you. I just raked.

Wislawa was still looking at the mountain. The water in her iron, upright on the table, gurgled. Through the party wall came the simmering noise of the neighbour's TV, a noise like voices talking in a saucepan.

I'm going to be earning very soon, Sucus said.

I'll believe that, son, when it happens.

I only need twenty-five thousand. Twenty-five. So I can buy a sphygmomanometer! With a sphygmomanometer I'm away!

What on earth do you want a thing like that for?

You don't know what it is, do you?

Wislawa was thinking about something else. Did this, this, this—she hesitated, searching for the word she wanted, and the lack of the single word made her heart howl for the loss of Branch—did this *vagabond* from Rat Hill love her son?

From the Greek, *sphygmo*, Maman, meaning pulse, the sign of life.

What, Sucus?

With this machine and a white coat like the quacks have at the hospital, you can make eight thousand a day on Alexanderplatz!

You ought to be ashamed of yourself, trying to profit from other people's suffering.

And dentists, what do they do?

You don't even know how to listen to somebody's blood pressure.

I'll learn in five minutes.

A regular job is what you need.

Regular! You do your ironing, you do your ironing and you see nothing. There aren't regular jobs any more. They've gone. There's no way. My poor Mother, it's like that, there's no way.

Wislawa laid another folded green tablecloth on the pile by the window. The neighbours were now watching a football match and it sounded as if the commentator was running for dear life as he shouted his commentary.

In a moment I'll make us something to eat, said Wislawa.

Is it true? asked Sucus, his eyes shut. Are there people in the village who live on a mountain so high up, so far away, that when they whisper they can hear an echo from the rocks?

There are places like that.

Sucus swung his feet up into the air as if he was going to walk on the ceiling and then, in one bound, stood upright on the still uncarpeted floor.

Why don't we go back to the village, Maman, the three of us?

Three of us?

You, Zsuzsa, and me. Father always said there was a wooden house on the mountain and a pine forest that still belonged to us. We could live there. I'd cut down trees, you'd keep chickens, and Zsuzsa, she'd gather mushrooms and sell them on the other side of the frontier, like the woman Father told us about, what was her name?

Why am I crying? Wislawa asked herself.

We'd grow our own vegetables, said Sucus, and in the winter I'd get work on the ski lifts, and in the summer I'd cut wood.

It's not like you think. There's no way, my boy, there's no way.

. . .

Sucus took the metro in the direction of Eddington. He got down at Piton and walked along the sea road towards the tanneries. The road was lit with yellow overhead lights like an auto route. When there were no trucks passing, Sucus could hear the waves breaking on the shingle. He could also smell the tanneries. There were more corrosive smells in Troy—the smell, for instance, of the fertiliser factory in Gentilly, but, in the dark, the smell of the tanneries made him think of catacombs. From *kata*, which meant down under in Greek. Down-under where Clement his father was.

When the road turned the headland Sucus's spirits rose, for he could see, quite near, the lights on Rat Hill. Like many people born in cities he was frightened of empty distance. He ran a little. Soon he heard radio music. Suddenly, all the lights he could see went out. Then they came on again. This happened several times. In the pitch darkness the hill of huts and shacks was like a sleeping dog, when the lights came on it was like a dancing bear. Some of the houses had strings of coloured lights strung along their walls. It was impossible for him to find his way, for at night all his familiar landmarks were lost. It was either a labyrinth of lights or as dark as a well. He stopped by the door of a hut where some kids were sorting into piles the salvage brought back by the garbage collectors: one pile for electrical fittings, another for women's shoes, another for medicines, another for large tins.

. . .

Do you know Uncle Dima's house? Sucus asked a boy who was smoking.

The Blue House! Zsuzsa's!

That's the one.

The boys gathered round him.

A beautiful knife you have there, hinny.

It's old, very old. It belonged to my father.

Can I see it? asked the one with the cigarette and dark circles under his eyes.

Sucus drew the knife out of its scabbard and held it up, the finger of one hand on its point and the other hand round its reindeer handle. In the light of the hurricane lamp in the hut the knife glinted like water.

Life is as thin as a sharpened blade. The rest is God.

Can I feel your shiv? asked the same boy.

Sucus shook his head.

I'll give you fifteen thousand for it.

Sucus shook his head again.

Twenty thousand!

It's not for sale.

Everything's for sale, hinny.

Tonight I haven't a sou, said Sucus, I'm telling you, I haven't a single sou, and I'm not selling my knife.

Because your Dad gave it to you?

The boy threw away his cigarette.

There are things you don't sell, said Sucus.

So you want to find Zsuzsa!

You're lucky, man, because we know her!

Zsuzsa and her zazzle!

To find Zsuzsa, said the one who wanted to buy, you follow the electricity cables, up and up, till you pass the second blind pig on your left.

You know what a blind pig is, I guess?

I wasn't born yesterday, said Sucus.

Nor was Zsuzsa!

How would you like Zsuzsa as a mum?

By the blind pig you turn right and it's the Blue House.

. . .

The house inside was as crowded with things as Rat Hill was crowded with shacks and people and children and poultry. There were clothes, saucepans, cardboard boxes, cushions, plates, bottles, shoes, towels, rags, jugs, a table, a mattress on the floor, a TV set, a wardrobe, a gas ring, a gas cylinder, a sink. Yet the room was full of arrangements and touches which showed that women lived there.

Where the gigantic mattress touched the wall, the pillows had been placed in a straight line under the cloth that served as a bedspread, and along this mound was laid a runner of white lace. The plates on the shelf fixed to a wall of naked briseblocks were carefully stacked in descending size, the largest at the bottom. In the centre of the cardboard ceiling a photo of a flying gull had been pasted; from the bed it looked as if it were flying towards you. Most noticeable of all, there were five mirrors in the small room! The largest, in a gilt frame the shape of a church window, was rested against the wall by the back of the sink. Its grey surface was spattered with black spots where the mercury had disappeared. It looked like the soil of Rat Hill, but if you stood by the sink, in its solemn dark reflection you could see your whole body.

Look at this! said Zsuzsa's mother, Kaja.

She held up the garment she was ironing by its shoulders. It was a tailored jacket, in black and white dog-tooth tweed. As she held it up, she couldn't resist swinging it as it would swing on a woman walking, tight across the shoulders, flared over the hips.

It's for Zsuzsa, she explained, she bought it this afternoon.

Smart, said Sucus.

There's a skirt goes with it.

She went on ironing around her large splayed-out left hand which held the jacket in place. Sucus noticed that on one of the lapels there was a hole, black at the edges, which must have been caused by a burn.

It's nothing! said Kaja, as if the weight of her ample, apple-brown body overflowing her violet cotton dress, could give such emphasis to the two words that the hole would disappear.

Did it happen ironing?

I'd say a burning coal fell on it, said Kaja.

How?

Must have thrown off her clothes by a fireplace to be fucked. Anyway, whatever happened, happened. If nothing had happened it wouldn't be here tonight. Rich ladies don't throw away tweed suits in perfect condition. It won't show if you get her some flowers to pin there.

Kaja winked.

Are you hungry? I'll heat some polenta for you. Naisi's out the back with the girl. Tell her to come in.

On Rat Hill there was no flat ground except where men dug to build. Every home on the slopes had begun with a spade and a shovel. Now that some families were richer they sometimes began by hiring Achille, who had lost a leg and owned a recuperated bulldozer. Behind the Blue House a plot of about four metres square had been levelled with pick and shovel by Uncle Dima before he went to prison. The idea was to build a room for Zsuzsa and Julia: then Uncle Dima and Kaja would be able to sleep alone in the room where the mirrors were. The second room was occupied at night by Naisi. To justify this regal privacy, Naisi called the room his

HQ. Since Uncle Dima's arrest, work behind the house had stopped. The tiny plot was strewn with wood Uncle Dima had collected for the construction—planks, palings, packing cases, an old telephone pole. These made it look as if the lean-to the family was dreaming of building had just collapsed. It was often difficult on Rat Hill to tell the difference between what was falling down and what was going up.

Naisi and Zsuzsa were sitting on a crate amongst the debris and Zsuzsa was listening to her brother. Naisi could read, but it wasn't books he read. He continually read the signs of what was happening on the hill and down in the city, of the new rackets of survival, and, best of all, of the latest plans for joining those for whom survival wasn't a problem. Naisi read all the while—which is why he considered manual work a waste of time. Everywhere he went, he read: people's characters, the way they lied, their fears, the city districts and the men who controlled them, the layout of buildings, rumours, new market prices, police reports, street maps—and when he wasn't reading, he was thinking about what he had just read. This is why, talking in the dark behind the house, Naisi looked as if he was teaching his sister something. He wasn't really. It was her way of listening and his way with words.

I wouldn't ask you to at night, Naisi was saying, I'm talking about afternoons, afternoons only . . .

Sucus approached. Your new suit's ironed, he said.

Flag, I want to be called Lilac, said Zsuzsa.

Lilac isn't a name.

It's the name of a flower and a perfume, and a tree.

It's not a woman's name. Lila! Lily! Lilith! But not Lilac.

Listen, the garbage man I bought my new rig from was

singing a song. It was written by a friend of his called Ottay
Rifat who lives on Tortoise. It goes like this.

Laying her head back, she sang:

> *On the corner of the street*
> *The lilac's in flower*
> *So I have to pray and implore*
> *Lilac, oh Lilac*
> *Oh let me pass by*
> *Lilac, my sweet . . .*

Further down the slope two dogs were barking.

Zsuzsa got to her feet, kissed Sucus on the lips, and went
inside the shack.

It's a bad sign when dogs bark at night. In the village they
say it's because they have heard something in the forest.

It's good you came, said Naisi. We've got to make some
new people. Ever made a new person?

Maybe we made one a few nights ago!

We need ten, Brother-in-Law.

Give us a few years!

We need ten by the day after tomorrow.

That's a lot.

With mugs, names, and numbers.

Papers?

Yes, international ones, we need passports.

Who's paying? Sucus asked.

We'll say I'm paying.

How much, Naisi?

Five hundred thousand for the ten.

You should tell him, Naisi, the one who's really paying, said Sucus, you should tell him he's making you look mean. Ten heists for five hundred thousand!

We've checked it out. It'll take you and Zsuzsa a quarter of an hour, at minimal risk.

All ten?

If you get more, we pay more. Budapest Station. Tomorrow night. Ten o'clock. Platform 17. Schlafwagen 101.

What are you going to do with the passports?

I told you, Sucus, we need some new people.

It was at this moment that Zsuzsa appeared wearing the dog-tooth suit. In the dark they could see she had changed and that a tight skirt ended just above her knees, but not much more than that. Yet the two of them went on gazing at her. Both men loved her. The barking of the dogs had stopped. Naisi straightened his shoulders and tapped on the earth with one of his boots to match his sister's elegance. If he was a reader, she was why he wanted to read. He loved her the way a musician can love an instrument, or a pilot his racing car. All he wanted was to entice the best from her, so as to give it back to her as her own pleasure. The pleasure of being Zsuzsa. He had known nothing in his life as beautiful, in his eyes, as his sister. There was no jealousy in Naisi's life, only this intimate, immense ambition.

Sucus loved her without any ambition. He loved her jealously, passionately, protectively.

Lilac, oh Lilac
Oh let me pass by . . .

he hummed, and Zsuzsa opened her arms.

I can hear the sound of a hunting horn. The hunting horn is strange, always leaving, its back turned, speaking over its shoulder. Everything about it announces departure. And the hunting horn is as male as the harp is female.

I hear the horn beneath the high glass roof of Budapest Station, on platform 17, and it's like the howling of a wild animal. I can almost touch the animal's fur, warm, sweaty, golden burrs lodged in it, thick as felt. The bellowing of its voice bruises itself against the cast-iron pillars, crying for the wounds and the wounded to come.

Sucus and Zsuzsa were walking down platform 17, one behind the other, and there was nothing to suggest they'd ever met in their lives. Nothing to suggest it because Sucus's thoughts were inaudible and invisible. He was thinking: In that skirt her legs look as tall as the sky! Yet I know where they end! His other thought was: Please God let it go well.

Zsuzsa was wearing her dog-tooth two-piece. On its lapel were pinned white dahlias Sucus had stolen that morning from a garden in Escorial. She was carrying a black canvas grip Naisi had supplied. It hung from her right shoulder, where buglers carry their bugles. Her hair was hidden in a white, Egyptian turban, which her grandmother had taught her how to put on.

A strip of fine cotton muslin, at least three metres long. You fold it until it is quite narrow, then wind it round your head, leaving two long ends hanging. These you braid tightly into a white plait which encircles your head like a halo.

In front of the dark mirror by the sink it had taken Zsuzsa half an hour to make the Egyptian turban, which pulled back and covered all her hair.

You look like Nefertiti, Naisi had said as she left the house; then he added: Don't worry about the grip, leave it if you have to. Schlafwagen 101. He's famous for his lechery!

Along with the turban, Zsuzsa was wearing a pair of dark sunglasses. There was nothing to be done about disguising her two missing teeth. She had varnished her finger nails blood red.

Sucus, following Zsuzsa, was wearing his father's raincoat. The label by the collar said Aquascutum. His father had explained the name to Sucus. Latin *aqua*, water. Latin *scutum*, shield. Clement had been given the raincoat by a restaurant owner for whom he had opened a thousand oysters at a banquet. A client had left it in the restaurant a year before and never come back. Wearing it, Sucus looked as though he had a regular job. Wislawa's heart, when she saw him trying it on that morning, had tightened with a kind of hope.

It was a TEN train. Trans Europe Night. It would cross the continent and reach the far ocean in three days. Schlafwagen 101 was a sleeper, with amber-coloured curtains already drawn across the high-up windows. Its coachwork was burgundy red. Down near the platform somebody had written with a white aerosol: SHIT TRUCK!

Zsuzsa walked slowly past, looking up through her black

sunglasses at the curtained windows and stopping once or twice so that the attendant should notice her. He did. She beckoned and he came to the door of his wagon. First, she handed him her luggage, then she stepped up herself. She was wearing white, flat-heeled plastic sandals, the cheapest kind, such as are sold at the beach, but the way she stepped up the steps with these sandals on her feet made them look handmade!

I was eleven when my grandmother taught me to scythe. Men sweat buckets, she said, and die young, so you'd better learn now. And learn I did. When your scythe is well hammered and the blade on it's sharp edge is so thin you can bend it with your thumbnail and the bright metal winks back at you, then scything is not a movement of your arms and shoulders, but of the hips, purely the hips. The grass knows when it's being cut by a young woman and not a man. And for a similar reason the TEN train knew when Zsuzsa stepped up onto it.

I'm travelling to Paris, she said to the attendant. So I have to spend two nights on your train.

The schlafwagen attendant was thinking: She's a cayack, an upper-class cayack.

Sucus, still on the platform, was watching the schlafwagen attendant talking to Zsuzsa at the top of the steps.

Let me explain, she continued confidentially, let me explain my dilemma to you.

It was Sucus who had suggested the word *dilemma* when they rehearsed that afternoon. *Dilemma* from the Greek *dis*, meaning two, and *lemma*, meaning that which has been taken in or perceived.

I'm sure you can help me, Mr. Schlafwagen Attendant. I just didn't have time to make a reservation. It was a last-minute decision, and now the prospect of two long nights without being able to undress and slip into bed would be too much! If you can find me a berth, I'll take your train. If not, I'll go by air!

Up there in the coach, above the platform, it was another world. Space was very confined. Two people could scarcely pass in the corridor, they had to squeeze by each other sideways and yet everything brushed against was classy, classy and intimate. Most of the passengers not already in bed were preparing for bed, hanging up their jackets, kicking off their hand-made shoes, taking off their Parisian scarves. Rich man's shanty train, thought Zsuzsa to herself.

The schlafwagen attendant, in his gold-braided, chocolate-coloured uniform, indicated the way to his bureau. From the table beside the sliding door with brass fittings he picked up his chart of reservations.

If you've no place, I'll get down . . . Can you help me make up my mind?

As it happens, Madame, there is a spare berth.

Wonderful! Could I see it?

This was the decisive moment. Would he or would he not walk her down the corridor immediately? Abruptly and cunningly she changed her look: she pouted, her mouth went hard. He rose to the challenge and he rose to the bait.

Follow me, Madame.

He led the way down the corridor and unlocked cabin

number 20. This berth was usually kept for last-minute arrivals who tipped well. But from the upper-class cayack the schlafwagen attendant was going to refuse payment in money. The lace bedspread on the bunk showed a flying dove surrounded by stars.

Luck is never indifferent; it's always either with you or against you. At that instant, the attendant, Zsuzsa, and Sucus all believed they were in luck. Sucus, because the attendant had left the sliding door of his bureau open. Zsuzsa, because the spare berth was at the other end of the coach. And the schlafwagen attendant, because when they crossed the frontier, he was going to get his ground rent.

Loudspeakers were announcing the departure in two minutes of the TEN train from platform 17.

Sucus slipped into the attendant's bureau and slid the door shut. It was no bigger than the crane cabin. The passports of the passengers who had gone to bed were neatly arranged in a pigeon-hole above the little table. He picked them, one by one like runner beans, and dropped them into the pocket of his raincoat. Then he slid the door back and walked casually down the corridor, like a man looking for a business colleague who has taken a stroll down the train. As he passed cabin number 20 he heard Zsuzsa exclaim: It's perfect!

Sucus climbed down onto the platform, deliberately leaving the coach door open so she would be able to jump down.

If you care to give me your passport, Madame, we can arrange the little formalities of the ticket later.

No problem, darling.

The attendant, dumbfounded by the thrill of hearing this word so soon, hardly noticed her squeezing past him fast as a ferret.

I must kiss Mother goodbye! She's waiting on the platform!

The train began to move. Sucus, alarmed that she had not yet appeared, was about to jump back on. But there she was in the doorway, triumphant. She landed on the platform as lightly as a magpie.

The schlafwagen attendant, on the steps of his wagon, shouted, with furious regret, as the train gathered speed:

Your luggage, Madame, your luggage!

In order not to draw attention to herself, Zsuzsa turned and waved at the departing train. When the other people began to drift away, she followed the crowd.

You got them? she whispered.

Fourteen.

Slowly he took her hand and put it inside his father's raincoat so she could touch the passports. She felt the whole wad of them. Then, smiling hard, she let her head fall from side to side like an idiot puppet. They both fell silent, suddenly exhausted. They were in a metro going north.

It goes through the mountains where my father came from, the TEN.

Faraway mountains, she said.

At the other end of the coach a man started to sing, standing up. He was singing not for his pleasure but for money.

Why don't we go there? asked Sucus.

Don't be stupid.

We could take tomorrow's train.

We could, yes.

We've got the cash.

First-class?

If you want, Lilac.

What would we do when we got there?

I've got a wooden house on a mountain.

You told me you'd never been there.

My father's house. High up on the cliff face, near a waterfall. We could live in it.

The metro stopped at Temple. Many people got on, among them two dwarfs who took the seats behind Sucus and Zsuzsa.

You said everything was milk in your father's village!

That's what he used to say. Milk's the only thing we have to sell in the village. If I heard it once, I heard him say it a hundred times.

The singer was now singing "Guantanamera."

Naisi says you milk goats.

He says whatever comes into his head.

It's not true?

Who knows?

You can kill chickens!

I can kill schlafwagen attendants!

Fourteen, Lilac. That makes seven hundred thousand.

Let's spend the night at the Hotel Patrai.

Where do you think it is?

It's beyond Chicago. You can see it from Rat Hill. Across the bay. A big place covered with turrets like a cathedral. Let's go there, Flag.

Behind them, the two dwarfs were also talking.

I'm nervous, said one of them to the other.

No need.

Suppose they drop us on the floor?

Can't happen, there's too many of them.

Suppose they toss us through a window!

Unlikely.

Are they young and strong?

Around your age, Samuel.

And the women . . .

They arrange the contests, if you ask me, for their women!

The women get excited. They love catching us, five, six, seven of them, holding the sheet out. When we bounce up we touch their tits. And they shriek.

The train stopped at Spallanzi.

How high do they throw us? asked Samuel, the younger dwarf.

As high as they can, up to the chandeliers.

I'm still nervous.

You can't expect to earn big money without a little risk.

I don't mind dancing . . .

It's they who do the dancing, Samuel, not us!

We do the falling! said Samuel.

"Guantanamera" came to an end and the singer walked down the aisle, cap in hand. Most of the passengers gave him a coin or two. The elder dwarf found his wallet and slowly drew out a bank note.

You're kings! Two kings! slurred the singer, who smelt of wine.

Sucus too pulled out a note. He had insisted that Naisi pay them half on rowing in, and half on delivery. He placed the note carefully in the man's cap. It was a way of saying thank-you.

. . .

To the north of Budapest Station lay Sankt Pauli, one of the city's red-light districts. It consisted of three parallel streets which, in the previous century, had been the quarter of the city's printers. Now the shopfronts and workshops and living quarters had been converted into bars, strip joints, sex shops, and rooms, hundreds of rooms. Prostitutes lined the three streets there from eleven in the morning. I can tell you how men in Troy referred to them: as cruisers, flatbackers, koorvas, hookers, bangtails. Birds in the hedges have prettier names. But some of their petnames suggested more tenderness: Squirrel, Lorraine Luv, Feather Duster, Luscious Lou. All of these women dreamt of another life, and in this they resembled most people on this earth, but they had a better reason.

At the top of the third street was the most famous and spacious bar of the district, called Flores. On the evening of the passports, Superintendent Hector was sitting in this bar drinking whiskey. He was in a sombre mood. He had left the station in Cauchy Street at eight, eaten in an Italian restaurant, and come on to Flores. He only came here when he was feeling low. He chatted with the girls, who treated him not like a client but like a Seigneur. They knew who he was. They needed to keep out of trouble. They wanted to ingratiate themselves with him, but they'd also been told that he never went with any of them and that he hated silliness. So they treated him like a Seigneur. And this was balm to his wounded soul. Tonight Feather Duster was talking to him:

So they took us out in their yacht, yes, they had a Paraguayan flag, you should have seen what it was like on board, hot showers, a cocktail bar, video, white leather settees, Swedish glass, we laughed fit to kill when one of them said to me: All I want is a tour of the world!

Superintendent Hector wasn't listening, he was thinking: In two weeks even the girls here will know I'm finished. When I come through the door, Winner may still say, A scotch, Superintendent, it's my pleasure! For a couple of months, maybe, he'll continue. Then one day, he'll say to himself, What the hell, let the old bastard pay for his own jolts. And the new girls will eye me and the old hands'll tell them, Let that one slide, honey, used to be a bogie, wants nothing, sits there to get a hard-on just watching us, never seen him offer a girl half a glass of bubbly . . . past it, we let him slide. Every day it's getting worse, the Superintendent told himself. If I walk out on Susanna, I'm going back, I'm going back to the village.

So we didn't return till Monday, Feather Duster was saying, it was quite a weekend! Though, to tell the truth, after two days it was nice to get ashore again and walk on solid ground.

Do you know where they were sailing afterwards?

To Izmir, they said.

What did they pay you in?

Superintendent Hector, is that a question I have to answer here in Flores?

Some champagne, Feather?

That would be nice, Superintendent . . . Dollars, they paid us in dollars, as a matter of fact.

A bottle of the Widow, said Hector.

When they raised glasses to one another, he looked into her eyes. They were unspiteful, insincere, generous. She looked into his and was surprised. She could see it coming before he knew it himself. He poured her another glass, the Superintendent wasn't drinking. Before she took a sip, his hand was on her thigh. A large peasant hand. Here it comes, she thought. His fingernails began to play like a child's in a fleece of wool.

Shall we go to my place? she asked when the bottle was empty.

Tell me your number. I'll join you there.

As she left, Feather Duster opened her eyes big and raised her eyebrows to the girls at the bar. Look what's got into the

bogie, her look said. The Superintendent followed her a minute later.

To get in, to find the way back. The urge is sometimes so
strong it will take the hand of anything—shit, piss, blood,
whatever is warm, whatever was at home inside. Inside:
where we were before we had to learn about life and were
thrown out.

He had to walk five doors down the street. He knew the
number. It was next to the Golden Fleece. He had a searing
pain in his heart. This pain would take any way back in, like
a blinded dog who had only its nose, it remembered a nameless
happiness. He climbed the stairs to the second floor. Feather
was already in her dressing gown.

Scythes! When I was young, I found it strange that they
cut as they do cut. Enough to strike a single stone, and the
blade's edge tears like a mouth with a tooth knocked out. The
scythe with its silvery edge and black shoulder is so close to
blood, far closer than a needle or an axe or a knife. It's so
close to blood because of the thinness of its blade. The thinness of a garment.

Inside the marble hall of the Hotel Patrai there was nothing except a lift made entirely of glass and framed by golden-coloured metal. Even the floor of the lift was made of glass. As soon as Zsuzsa and Sucus entered the lift, its doors closed and they started to ascend, like the Madonna of the Cherubs into the sky, visible from every side.

The whole world can see us! giggled Zsuzsa. You're sure you've got the smash?

Sucus nodded. Then he tapped the glass.

Bulletproof, he said.

When the lift at last stopped, they found themselves in another large hall, this one carpeted and wood-panelled. There were some small trees in tubs and two or three suits of armour.

Not a soul, said Zsuzsa.

It's one o'clock!

To their surprise, at the reception desk at the far end of the hall sat an old woman rather like myself. She wore black, she had worn hands with arthritic knuckles, her forearms, if they could have seen them, were weathered, and the rest of her body, if they could have seen it, was very pale.

You require a room? she asked, looking at the register.

With a bathroom and a view onto the sea, said Sucus.

You have no luggage? remarked the old woman.

We left it at the airport, said Sucus.

We're flying out tomorrow, said Zsuzsa, waving her sun-glasses, so we only brought our—

Of course, said the old woman.

To Rio de Janeiro, added Zsuzsa.

Where else? said the old woman.

We'd like something to eat in the room, said Sucus.

I'll send up my grandson to take your order. If you'd be so good to sign here, sir, and settle for the room immediately.

Sucus hesitated. It is difficult to invent a name for yourself on the spur of the moment. All names flee except the one given you by your parents. Finally, he invented Murat Ioannide.

The room is one hundred thousand, said the old woman.

Zsuzsa was looking at one of the suits of armour. Each finger-piece could bend three times. Over the breast the metal was finely engraved. Where his sex was, it made a shape like a small cake tin.

Why not champagne, darling? she proposed, looking straight into the visor.

My grandson will bring up a bottle.

Chilled, said Sucus.

As chilled as the bottle Boris kept in the trough of his yard before he died.

I don't understand . . .

No, no, how could you? It was a village story. Here's the key to your room, sir. On the third floor.

The room was far larger than the Blue House and the levelled ground behind it. Yet it was almost empty. Zsuzsa stood in the doorway transfixed. From the high ceiling hung a chandelier with strings of cut glass. In places, bits of glass were missing and you could see the bulbs. As one of the strings turned, traces of light shot all over the room. Between the two bay windows there was a television, and along half of one wall an immense wardrobe. The varnish had mostly worn off the floorboards which were the colour of grey sand. It was the bed that surprised her most. Neither of them had seen a four-poster before. It had a tattered canopy of yellowish silk, the colour of the bars on the wings of a goldfinch. Around the borders of the whole ceiling, acanthus leaves were modelled in deep white plaster.

What are we going to do, Flag?

Go in and shut the door.

They went in. Zsuzsa stepped out of her shoes and went round the room, touching things. The four posts, the goldfinch canopy, the lace runners on the bedside tables, the handles to the six doors of the wardrobe. She drew the velour curtains of the two windows and looked out into the night.

Once the Hotel Patrai with its private beach had been fashionable with the English, but oil from the tanking station further up the coast had polluted the sea, and now where the bathing huts had once been, there was a hovercraft station. All Zsuzsa could make out was a floating landing stage.

She lit the television and, pulling up her skirt like a whore, she sat astride it. Three cowboys rode between her legs. One fell off his horse. A sheriff entered a bar. Her two brown legs either side of the screen made the highly coloured actors look like toys.

She turned off the TV with her toe and went into the bathroom where the bath had rust stains and brass taps. There she played with the lights, switching them on and off by pulling a cord with a tassle. She came back and sat on the edge of the bed. Now the immense room, and the furniture and the fabrics from another century and another empire, were hers for the night. She took a large pillow and clutched it to her chest, smiling.

Let's look at the passports, she said.

Sucus handed them to her and she arranged them in a pile on the top of the television. She opened the top one, examining the photograph.

A man, she said. She looked closer. Not one I'd trust.

She handed the passport to Sucus.

He's American. From Carolina. Born 1957. Has blue eyes.

Any children?

Two.

Do they live with him?

Doesn't say.

What does he do?

It says Federal Police.

He's a scuffer?

That's what it says.

I told you not to trust him, didn't I? I can see through people, Flag. Like I saw through you in a flash, outside St. Joseph's. I saw you were good, I saw you were going to be the man of my life. So I don't have to read, do I? If I could read, I wouldn't know more.

She picked up the next passport and studied it. You have to guess, she said. Man or woman?

Man.

No. Woman. How old is she?

Forty?

No, she's my age. What colour is her hair?

Blond.

Wrong again. It's black like mine.

Zsuzsa placed the passport face down on the TV.

Now for the big question. Think carefully. Is she beautiful?

No, she's not beautiful at all.

You're wrong, she's very beautiful. She's wearing a dog-tooth jacket, no burns, and pinned to it, there's a brooch worth ten million.

Whilst saying this, she stretched one leg, then the other,

and began to dance slowly past the windows. Sucus turned over the passport she had left lying face down. The small photo showed a bald man in his fifties!

She stopped dancing to watch his reaction. For a fraction of a second, before he bellowed, he looked lost, utterly lost. And at that instant she loved him more than she had ever done.

I think they've forgotten our supper, is what she said.

He took the lift down to the reception hall. There was a light by the counter. Near the telephone exchange a green eye was blinking. Otherwise everything was still. The old woman was fast asleep on a settee by the wall. Above the settee was a large poster announcing the films being shown in Troy that week. He tiptoed behind the counter. In the upright pigeonholes, below the hooks for the room keys, stood several passports. He hesitated. Walked round the hall. Tried the doors of a bar and the dining room. Tried the double glass doors of the lift with the word PATRAI written on them in gold. They were locked. No, he decided, no passports.

Zsuzsa sat cross-legged in the middle of the bed, beneath the goldfinch canopy, waiting for him. In the book of pictures I found in the presbytery the day Monsieur Le Curé Besson came back sooner than expected and closed the book like a shutter, the same book where I found the picture called "Roman Charity," there was another, which I will remember for ever. It showed the Queen of Sheba in her tent. Outside it was night, the stars in the sky a reminder of how short life is. The entrance to the tent, which was the colour of coral with cream trimmings, was wide open, its canvas flaps drawn back and held in two loops like curtains. The queen's face was solemn and amused. I think she wanted to be solemn, but she could feel the laughter coming! She sat there in her tent, holding her hands tight between her knees. Zsuzsa, sitting on the bed, reminded me of Sheba.

She pulled off her Egyptian turban without untying it. Her dark hair sprang up, alive, glistening. Women everywhere, since the beginning of time, washing their hair, brushing, transforming to a glory, combing, platting, curling. It's the only thing, hair, along with bird's feathers, that is both apparel and nature. Its lights speak of this: they speak of silk, birds, water, fire, filigree, stars, rags, and dreams. There was a red line across Zsuzsa's forehead where the folded muslin had been pulled too tight.

The door opened and Sucus returned.

Zsuzsa made room for him on her throne. The centre of the world was now the two of them. If the earth quaked, they would both tremble. When the sun shone, they would lie in the sunshine together.

The old woman's fast asleep and everything's shut, he said.

Never mind.

No grandson there. Like I told you, she's got a few pages stuck together, the old lady.

No, no, she has her reasons, Flag. I knew there was no grandson. That's why I ordered champagne. She invents him and makes him a waiter, see? There aren't any waiters around the hotel when she arrives. She's by herself. So she invents this grandson for company.

And we've got nothing to eat!

People tell lies to feel less on their own. Lies do that. They keep you company.

She got off the bed and walked slowly across the room in her bare feet towards the wardrobe. Take Naisi, she said, half of what he says is untrue. But if he didn't invent, he wouldn't last a minute. He'd drown in his loneliness. She opened one of the wardrobe doors. Inside was a mirror. He invents for me too. I play along because—who knows?—what he invents may turn out to be true. But I always know what I'm doing. Never forget that, Flag. There are so few people on this earth who know what they're doing. They kid themselves. They say things for company. But I know. I know. You're hungry, my poor Flag. You can eat me! Remember what I told you the first day we met—you're going to eat me for ever and ever, Flag. She opened a second door of the wardrobe.

Tomorrow I'll buy the sphygmomanometer, said Sucus.

Are you sure? I'm not sure.

I'm dead sure.

We need piles of lettuce, Flag.

Think how much we made tonight!

We invented something tonight, didn't we?

You were famous.

Do you know what? I'm going to love you even more when you're fat. She was looking at herself in one of the wardrobe mirrors.

Me fat!

Fat. When we get some lettuce. Then you'll get fatter. Maybe I'll get fatter with fewer worries. What would you say if I was fat like Maman?

Never . . .

The interior of the wardrobe had to be touched to be believed. Its wood hadn't come from forests but from orchards: cherry, pear, walnut, peach. As large as one of our greniers, it had been made as carefully as a piano. In it would hang or lie folded the clothes of a lifetime. There were shelves, rails, drawers, racks, golden rods, and a small glass box like an aquarium.

What did they keep there? Zsuzsa asked herself. And suddenly she knew what she would keep there: peaches! The coat-hangers were padded and covered with satin.

I like men with tummies, she said, a little purse to pinch here, a little purse to pinch there . . .

She took off her jacket and put it on the hanger, then she wriggled out of her skirt. Her panties were of cheap black lace.

I'm not going to wear the same rig two days running, Flag. Tomorrow I'll wear my jersey dress for you. It's pinkish grey and sleeveless and you can see my back right down to where my arse begins. The shoulder straps are pearly, all stuck with sequins. I'll wear it with silver stockings. Are you listening, Flag?

As an old woman I love lace. I can spend hours looking at lace. It shows me how there is order in what is undone, that nothing can be hidden, that everything is joined by threads. I see all this when I'm looking through the lace curtains. But I love it most on a body, when there's flesh glowing through it and the lace and the skin tease each other with what is missing! The last stitches worn . . .

Or do you want me to wear my panther dress tomorrow? It's imitation, Flag, made of wool. Made of jersey, like the grey one next to it, but it's much tighter fitting and its black spots are like paw marks—as if . . . as if he stood on his hind legs and leant against me!

The wardrobe was empty.

You like my feather boa, Flag? Look! It's orange and green!

As she said this, she was unbuttoning the poplin shirt she had lifted a month before from an Argonaut supermarket.

It must be a hundred years old, this bed, said Sucus.

It's for getting married in, she said.

She folded her shirt and placed it on one of the pearwood shelves in the empty wardrobe.

You don't want to see my dowry, Flag?

The posts are all carved, he said.

With leaves.

Yes, vine leaves.

No, fig leaves, said Zsuzsa.

You think I don't know the difference between a vine and a fig.

Fig leaves! And after you've been married in a bed like that, one day you have a baby in it, she said.

Boy or girl? asked Sucus.

She hesitated. Girl.

What'll we call her? Sucus laid his head back on the pillows.

Zsuzsa hesitated again. Jeanne, she said and stepped into the wardrobe as though it were a phaeton to carry her away.

There is only one horse left in the village and it is owned by Jeanne. Jeanne is not her real name but everybody calls her Jeanne because many years ago, when she was young and beautiful, she played the part of Jeanne d'Arc riding a white horse in the village procession on the occasion of the five hundredth anniversary of the saint's death. Hercule, the young road-mender, fell in love with her. And she married him because he was upright and strong. He could carry tree trunks of several hundred kilos across his shoulders without slackening his pace. As the years went by Hercule began to drink. It was as if his strength became thirsty, and then the roads he mended became thirsty, till finally his memories drank too. Jeanne became the saviour of their farm and of their six cows. Today her horse is grey and thirty years old. Scarcely a day passes when Jeanne doesn't harness him and take him out to work. Even when there is deep snow, she uses him to pull the triangle that clears the road to their farm. Hercule, suffering from thrombosis of the legs, is nearly bedridden. The most he can do is to walk a hundred metres in his carpet slippers to the drinking trough and feed the chickens. With her horse, Jeanne works the fields, using farm machines which, in the age of tractors, are unfindable anywhere else. From afar, riding her tipcart, she and the horse look like ghosts. Near to, when you see her broad brown face, the colour of leather, and the fury in her eyes, you realise it is a woman you have met on the road.

Yes . . . Jeanne, repeated Zsuzsa from inside the wardrobe.

Through the tall bay windows of the immense room came the faint sound of a ship's siren. It was a large ship, far away.

We've never spent a whole night together, have we, Flag?

The voice in which she said this, quietly, and yet as if she wanted each word to be so distinct it would carry across the sea like an answer to the ship's horn, made Sucus lift his head from the pillow.

She was standing inside the wardrobe, framed by its two open doors. And she was naked. She was wearing only her earrings, each one big enough to pass a lemon through.

It's as familiar to us as bread is, or the sky. It seems we've known it without a name all our lives. We start trying to find a name for it, very young, on the way to the village school. We ask the statue of the Madonna, we ask the cows, and the moon, but none of them can give it a name. Old woman that I am, I still don't know its name. All I know is how it goes through us. Some of us more than others, but, even if only for a moment, it passes through all of us. Sometimes scarcely noticed. Sometimes remembered for ever. It's a kind of power. But not the power men pump themselves up with.

Perhaps this is why it has no name. It goes through us and joins us with the beginning of everything. It offers us the earth, more than the earth, the sky, heaven. When it's happening we know it. We know it in our tubes and our knees, our hips and the palms of our hands. We become desirable. The man's desire follows. Yet they can never begin it. They haven't the invention. Each time they have to begin with one of us. Then, all that has happened is forgiven. We become love. This is why they hate us, those with power. They hate forgiveness. Whilst its happening, time stands still. Later in our lives, time takes its revenge on us, as it doesn't on men. It can't forget that something in us once forced it to stop. When all is forgiven, there's no more place for power or time. So they glare with hatred at our love.

As she stood there naked in the door of the wardrobe, Zsuzsa felt this nameless thing running through her. She wanted, more than she had ever wanted anything, to share its promise with Flag. The swinging of her two earrings showed that she was moving. Her whole body was flickering, and yet she appeared to be standing quite still.

Sucus sat bolt upright and then, leaning forward on his arms, walked on all fours across the bed towards her.

She let her arms hang loose. Her body was dancing inside but she wanted to stay still. She wanted every hair and every piece of herself that had grown since she was a woman to be there before Flag's eyes. Slowly, she raised a hand. She had large hands, Zsuzsa. She touched her belly and then cupped one of her tiny breasts as an offering to him.

Love treasures hands like nothing else. Perhaps other parts are more cherished, more kissed, more dreamt of, but hands are treasured like nothing else, because of all they have taken, made, given, planted, picked, fed, stolen, caressed, arranged,

let drop in sleep, offered. At the very end of his life it would
be Zsuzsa's hands Sucus would be looking for.

She walked towards the bed. Together they took off his
clothes. Soon the slight stirring of the four carved posts broke
a few more threads of the tattered goldfinch canopy and the
few grains of silk dust that fell on them were golden.

. . .

They were talking in the dark. They lay in one another's
arms and I heard their voices. In the wardrobe mirror there
was a dim reflection of the window that looked over the sea.
Otherwise I could see nothing. They spoke in whispers.

Come into the tent.

I am.

My poor Flag.

Lilac.

Shall we go?

We could, you know.

Take a sleeper to Paris.

No, no, the big sleeper out.

Far, far away.

My nose in your cunt.

Your nose in my cunt.

One-way tickets!

First-class, and not in a shanty train.

Nobody'll notice.

We can't yet. Your mother! Give me time to fill our
wardrobe.

Wardrobe my arse!

It's too soon.

You want to be older? When I saw my dad in hospital I
said—

Come closer.

There'll be nothing better.

Better than what, love?

This.

They'd separate us and take everything away from us.

I'd find you in secret and pass you things through the bars.

My poor Flag.

If not now, when? If not here, where? I remember his words.

Whose words? Was he talking about love?

No, it was Murat. He was talking about the future.

With me!

With my nose in your cunt.

Yes, yes . . .

They murmured like babies feeding and falling asleep. The next time they spoke their voices came from the foot of the bed.

I'm the tent, I'm the tent!

Open, tent!

It's night.

Is there a moon?

I can see you in the dark.

Oh, now!

They made the purring noise that women and men make and which ends in a howl like a ship's siren, like dogs barking, like a hunter's horn, like an old woman crying. Then they went quiet. The wood of the bed creaked.

Are you awake, Flag?

Is it morning?

No.

Is it still dark?

Keep your eyes closed and I'll tell you.

Probably it was his eyes she was kissing. Anyway, she was kissing him. Then she said:

Everything's white, Flag, white, white like the walls of this room where we are marrying each other.

Hold me now.

selling

I have lived all my long life in the village. What I know of Troy comes from *The Messenger*—the provincial newspaper—from television, from my dreams, from my broken heart, and from what those who come back tell me before they disappear for good. I have seen countless men go. They take the noon bus outside the Republican Lyre and they wave through the back window as the bus winds its way down the hill past the dairy. This is the first and easiest step they take. Once they have left the valley and are far from the blue waters of our river—until they become Trojans, if ever they do—there is nothing in the world they can trust or depend upon. They are obliged to become like Fox or Hare.

Sucus bought his machine for taking blood pressure. No sooner was he out of the shop with the box under his arm than a man tapped him on the shoulder. He tapped hard from behind, like a knocker taps on a door. Surprised, Sucus turned round.

You want a tutor? asked the man.

He wore a large felt hat and he was well-dressed. His hands were clean. But he had a face that was slipping sideways, as if running out of its mould.

No, Sucus said, I don't.

You won't be able to operate alone, not in this line. The man indicated the cardboard box with two snakes printed in blue beneath the letters MANO and METER. You need a tutor.

I don't, said Sucus, I can learn in five minutes.

But you need a buyer.

A buyer to buy what?

Blood, my boy, blood. You're in the blood business, aren't you?

I read people's blood pressure, it's simple.

You talk about it like a book. I read! I read! If you want to read, here's my card. Take it, and read it.

He handed Sucus the card with an absolute surety as if nothing else in the city existed except the little white cardboard rectangle.

I draw off and I buy, he declared.

On the card was written ZIA MEDICAL APPLIANCES, followed by an address in San Isidro.

It's a new scam for you, you're a beginner!

I wasn't born yesterday, said Sucus.

I want a coffee, said the man in the large felt hat. I'll explain the ground plan over a cup of coffee.

Instead of counting as a weakness, the disfigurement of

his fallen face with its one drooping eye supplied him with a kind of conviction. All the niceties of life had fallen away since he was struck by his illness.

Due espressi! he commanded of a waitress in a coffee bar. Cheesecake?

No.

You don't eat, young man, because you're not earning enough.

I eat when I'm hungry.

Taking a customer's blood pressure is dead easy, he explained, provided you're not deaf. You don't look deaf to me. You look as if you want to hear. Do you want to hear?

You're doing the talking.

Some cheesecake?

Zia started to eat his own portion, sticking it with a fork and then biting voraciously from it with his teeth.

You pump up, he said, and you're listening for where the silence stops and starts. You follow me? The heart goes quiet. Where it starts and stops are what you call your fucking readings. You talk like your father was a teacher.

My father opened oysters.

For your two readings you get one thousand five hundred. Price of two coffees in a nice Italian bar like this. No more. And you're throwing a golden chance away! You're missing what's under your nose. Cheesecake?

Zia had finished his first portion and was about to order another. He wiped his lips with a folded handkerchief.

Do you know what I'm talking about? I'm talking about blood. What the old heart pumps! What keeps the brain connecting, what makes Old King Cole go big. You get it? I sell blood. You could be one of my suppliers. I'm offering you the chance of a lifetime. I pay my suppliers eight thousand per litre drawn off.

So, you're proposing to buy my blood, said Sucus with a smile.

What did you do before this? asked Zia.

I did flowers, said Sucus.

Wreaths and all that?

White dahlias.

Okay. You don't want to tell me. In this line you learn to misread, see? When you get a healthy client, you read wrong, you read a bit higher. Then you're obliged to warn him, or to warn her—women are easier, because they're more used to blood, more used to losing it. *Hypertension* is the key word. Hypertension causes varicose veins, strokes, clots, thrombosis, migraines, amnesia, blindness. It can ruin the retina of the eye. The client looks worried. Are there any medicines? she wants to know. You don't lie. You never lie. Some cheesecake? All right, you don't eat. I have to eat. I need blood sugar. Yes, you tell her, there are medicines but they're pricey! There's a much simpler and healthier way, you say. Works like a safety valve! Her blood pressure is way up, you tell her, because she's got too much blood, she's too healthy! Being too healthy always gets a laugh out of them! Nature's own safety valve, you insist . . . All they need is a little blood drawn off. And you can arrange it, especially for Monsieur, or especially for Madame, straightaway, no sooner said than done.

Who does the drawing off?

One of my nurses does. You bring the client.

How much do you pay?

Eight thousand a litre. I told you.

No, to the client.

If you've done your work properly, she or he believes she's getting free treatment! They think they're getting something for nothing. I've got three surgeries. One in Chicago, one off Alexanderplatz, and one by Olympia. Open every day between two and ten at night.

Do I get a retainer?

You refused it, my friend, three times. You didn't want any cheesecake. Think it over. *Quanto fa, Signorina?*

. . .

That afternoon Sucus practiced listening for the two silences on Zsuzsa. She rolled up her sleeve and he wound the elastic wrapping around her long, thin arm. The right arm. He loved her arms like other men love money. They promised everything he could imagine.

They were in the Blue House, sitting on the mattress on the floor, with the lace over the pillows. He placed the little black disc on her artery, in the crook of her arm. Now he could hear her heart reverberating like a pile driver and the sound made him smile. He pressed the rods of the stethoscope further into his ears.

Across the room, the door to Naisi's HQ was open and Naisi was lying on his bed with his eyes shut, calculating.

Zsuzsa, are you there? he asked. You haven't forgotten the audition tomorrow at three?

How could I? she replied.

Don't let it mess your mind, he said.

Sshhh! hissed Sucus, stop talking! I can't hear.

Am I making you go deaf, Flag? Too many beats?

Be quiet! I can't hear. There! It's gone quiet. Thirteen. Now for the lower one. The d-i-a-stol-ic . . .

No need to be worried, sister, said Naisi, it's only a gazupie, nothing more.

Sshh! It's eight!

Later, Sucus and Zsuzsa strolled down Rat Hill towards
the headland. It was sunny, with the special light of an
autumn afternoon, when everything cast such dark and long
shadows that the earth, and all that was standing on it, looked
as if it was slipping towards the sun. The wind was blowing
the stench of the tanneries out to sea. The washing, hung
out since the morning, was already dry. Hens sat drowsy in
the shade. Nobody was queuing up with plastic containers
at the hydrants because, since September, water had been
cut off every afternoon between three and six. In the blind
pigs, only the damned were drinking. There was an autumn
calm over the shanty town. Against the sky, the television
aerials at the top of the hill looked like the shipwrecked masts
of a fleet of toy boats.

They passed a girl on the path practicing with a hula hoop,
trying to keep it up on her hips. Zsuzsa stopped to show her
how to do it, then ran after Sucus and, pressing herself
against him, did her disappearing trick.

She's gone, she whispered in his ear, you won't find her
if you turn round, she's gone! For ever!

She knew that pressing herself like this against the back
of his legs excited him, and today she found it funny. His
joke was getting bigger. She laughed, neighing through her
nostrils on the nape of his neck, where his hair needed cutting. He looked like a mooch. She must cut it for him before
he began on Alexanderplatz. Bigger and bigger grew his joke,
and his ears were going red too. Suddenly, she sidestepped,
ran in front, and turned to face him. Her brass earrings, the
ones big enough to pass a lemon through, were swinging like

church bells at a wedding. I love you, she said, and kissed him. He lifted her off the ground.

And I weep, as old women do, seeing everything beginning again and remembering.

. . .

It was a mystery why there were always so many people on Alexanderplatz. There was the bus station, but this couldn't explain the crowds at night. Perhaps people went there simply because it was so big. Perhaps the bare, empty space, which was not like that of a park, compelled crowds to gather there, according to some natural law of men and streets and Man. All cities have one such space, where victories are celebrated, where crowds dance at the new year, where political marches begin and end, a space that belongs to the people, just as the buildings with pillars and carvings belong to the rich. When you cross it, it's like crossing a stage. On this stage, in times of summary justice, tyrants and traitors are hanged from lamp posts. The eternal audience are the poor, all the poor of the past and all the poor of the future, among whom there are many who go straight to heaven, if you want an old woman's opinion.

The kiosks and stands around the edge of the great open space sold newspapers, Coca-Cola, silver spoons, scarves, furry animals, cassettes, T-shirts with I ♥ ALEXANDERPLATZ printed on them, saffron, cameras, lace lingerie, cowboy hats, posters, toy buses like the real ones in the bus station, wigs, beer, sunflower seeds, electronic calculators. And the crowds were as diverse and strange as the things to be bought. Telling the difference between the villagers who had just arrived by bus, and those who had come generations ago was easy. It was enough, if they were men, to look at their footwear, and, if they were women, to look at their hair. A question of thickness in both cases. The Trojans believed in thin, fine things.

A massive bronze statue with a fountain dominated the western end of the platz. Around this statue flew and alighted hundreds of pigeons, attracted by the vendors who sold packets of grain for visitors to feed them with.

The statue was of a sailor standing on a rock talking to an Aegean mermaid. She was Aegean because her tail divided into three. The sailor's head was covered with lime from the pigeons, and this made his hair grey. The mermaid was protected from the bird shit since water flowed all over her, but the water had turned the bronze of her body green. According to legend, she was asking the sailor: Where is the great Alexander? And the sailor, according to legend, always told the mermaid: He lives and he reigns!

Nobody knew where. But the fountain was reproduced on hundreds of souvenirs—from rubber car mats to women's brooches. It was at the foot of the bronze sailor that people, if they failed to meet in the crowd, would find each other.

Was the statue so famous because it offered a consolation concerning death? Alexander died, burnt out, in Babylon at the age of thirty-two; and yet, after twenty-four centuries, the green mermaid still wanted news of him!

Sucus arrived early in the morning with a folding chair which Naisi had given him. Naisi had six of these chairs stacked in a corner of his HQ. They had disappeared from the private beach of the Hotel Atlantic during a storm.

Sucus chose a pitch within sight of the other blood-jobbers, but somewhat closer to the statue. He judged that he would be able to observe things better from there. He slipped on his white coat, unfolded the chair, and sat down, the sphygmomanometer across his knees and the stethoscope round his neck. A few passersby glanced at him, a few scowled, none stopped.

At the end of Alexanderplatz, where the buses were, a man sat on the ground, his back to a tree, against which two crutches were leaning. Arranged on the earth around him like a fan lay copies of the revolutionary newspaper *Milestone*.

Always thin, Murat looked even thinner. His face had become a mask hiding another world. When passengers got down from the buses, he looked up and repeated: *Milestone*! Two hundred zloti! *Milestone*! The front-page headline read: TROJAN WORKERS REFUSE INTIMIDATION!

Murat believed humanity would advance towards a juster future he would not live to see. Perhaps his children would. If not them, his grandchildren. Meanwhile people had need of *Milestone*'s message. Whenever he arrived at this thought, he did his best to sell the paper by crying out its name. The rest of the time, seated on the ground, lost in the immensity of his compassion, he watched the feet of the people passing.

If Murat had known that, a hundred metres away, Sucus in a white coat was waiting for clients who never came, he would have taken up his crutches and gone to share his thoughts with the young worker who had saved his life.

Nothing is more improbable, he would have told Sucus, than the way we walk. I've learnt this, now that I'm a cripple. The foot moves with great independence and yet is helpless alone. One leg goes as far as it can, then, almost immediately, it has to stop, it has to wait for its partner to relieve it. I watch all day between the buses. Forgotten knees—the most ignored part of the body until they hurt or refuse to flex— forgotten knees flexing, legs bravely striding out, waiting for relief, striding out again, waiting, striding out—and this every two seconds in order to move a body, step by step, across the earth. I watch them between the buses, Newborn. The one-legged man is worse off than the man without legs at all. Sit with me, you'll learn how the feet of a mother running after her child, smack the ground. How the feet of old men implore the tarmac. How the feet of the hungry shuffle. How porters' feet move slowly to earn their living. The poor use their toes, the rich don't. Hands are continually feeling for other hands. But the foot is singleminded, obstinate, dumb, attentive to only one thing—the arrival and passing of its partner. Like this mankind goes forward . . .

But Murat did not know his young friend was so near. After several hours Sucus got up, went to a kiosk, and bought two sheets of writing paper. On one side he wrote in large letters: HIGH BLOOD PRESSURE = HIGH RISK and pinned the sheet to his white coat. Nobody stopped.

After an hour he turned the sheet over and wrote: BE GOOD TO YOUR BLOOD. An old man in boots without laces came up and said, Yours is young! Sucus got to his feet. Fuck you! said the man. Nobody else stopped.

Sucus unfolded the second sheet of paper and wrote: A TEST IN TIME SAVES YEARS. People passed, eyes averted, nobody stopped.

On the last side he wrote: ONLY 1000 ZLOTI!

Within five minutes a young boy pulled at his sleeve and hissed, On Alexanderplatz no price-slashing unless you want your fucking face slashed!

Sucus raised his eyebrows without betraying any expression. The boy, teeth clenched, nodded in the direction of the other blood-jobbers. Sucus spat on the ground, packed his instruments, took off his white coat, folded up his chair and followed the ambling crowd.

He came to the statue of the sailor and the fountain. The water flowing over the mermaid's breasts as she asked for news of the Great Conqueror made Sucus think of Zsuzsa wanting to call their daughter Jeanne. If their child was a boy, he decided, they would call him Alexander. The more opportunities are taken away from men, the more they dream of being fathers.

On the spot, only a few paces from the statue, Sucus unfolded his chair and stood up on it. His instruments at the ready, he surveyed the crowd. He spotted a group of well-dressed sightseers with cameras. They were buying grain to feed the pigeons.

Hey, lady! Hey, lady-in-the-hat! he shouted, I'll do you for nothing, and your friends can watch. Come and see. Takes two minutes. Roll up your sleeve, lady. Don't be shy—you shouldn't be shy with shoulders like yours! Do you suffer from migraines? I do. And I'm telling you, here's the answer! Let me read your blood pressure—systolic and diastolic—names like music, aren't they? I'm offering you a test, I'm offering you a reading.

A pigeon alighted on his outstretched arm.

I'm offering you a free check-up, let me take your blood pressure!

She glanced at him for a fraction of a second, and he read in her eyes that it wasn't a blood test she wanted. The pigeon flew off his arm.

Let me listen to your heart, lady, and I'll tell you your future . . . I'll tell you whether it's going to be better or worse. You want to know, lady, where the great Alexander is?

Somebody tapped on his thigh. He looked down and saw Raphaele, the portrait-man, goggling up at him.

Last place I expected to see you, said Raphaele.
And you're still painting the ceiling?
You never kept your promise, jammy.
I promise nothing.
You promised to come round—in exchange for the drawing
I gave you. I told you I wanted to draw your trouser snake,
didn't I?
Get lost!
I'll tell you something, jammy, I'll give you a tip. You
haven't chosen the right pitch for your particular art here.
You'll never make it on Alexanderplatz. You look too young
for medicine. You'd have to grey your hair. Try around the
Sankt Pauli. The custom's less choosey down there. They
just want to hear if they can last the night. Without your
white coat though. Hospital around Sankt Pauli means punishment, it doesn't mean care. Down there, with no white
coat, you'd have a chance.

I saw the marten this morning. He was running. He never
runs blindly. He considers each mound in the garden before
he jumps over it or skirts around it. When he skirts around,
he keeps very low to the ground. Pointed, slim, and the colour
of a flame. As cunning as he's quick. It was three months
since I'd seen my marten. Where he lives I don't know, but
it can't be far from the house. We live side by side but invisible
one to the other. When our paths do cross, it's the result of
an accident or a mistake. This morning he was being pursued
by a dog. The marten, his skull as thin as a hen's egg, is a
sign of danger.

$\boxed{\text{T}}$he day was young. The fortunate who had jobs were going to work, the roads into Troy were crammed with traffic, those still in bed were mostly there alone, many dreaded the new day, the sun dazzled the sea. In the Cauchy Street police station the Superintendent was leaning back in his revolving chair, listening to a man whom he didn't want to see. Hector's appearance was changing for the worse. His face was becoming puffier and the backs of his hands with their black hairs were swollen. When I looked into his eyes, I had the impression that the tides of the sea were flowing through them, that he was adrift. It was his last week of work.

So, how did you know who it was? he asked his visitor.

I'm used to seeing people, the man said, I do it all day long.

Hector nodded and looked up blankly at the framed portrait of the President above the door.

The question came to my mind as soon as I spotted her, continued his visitor.

The question?

Is this woman a terrorist? It's not a thing I usually ask myself. I'm not a Police Superintendent like you. But there was something about this woman—his hand searched in the air for a word—which impelled me to ask it.

Where do you work?

At the Job Distribution Centre in Swansea. I'm due to retire at the end of the year.

It happens to us all, said Hector.

I can't wait, said the man.

So you thought she was a terrorist?

Yes, I didn't know *who* she was then. I just thought she was a terrorist.

So?

It was the way she was sitting.

Do terrorists sit in a special way?

The man on the other side of the desk now felt in his jacket pocket and produced a box of sweets which he held out to the Superintendent.

Since I gave up smoking, I eat these, would you like one?

Inside the box, the sweets were like brightly coloured leggo bricks with which, if you had enough of them, you could probably build a spaceship, or a telephone booth. Their colours were lemon-yellow, gold, rose-pink, black, mahogany-red.

No thank you, said Hector.

Inside they're licorice.

Suddenly Hector thought of heroin. Who would think of looking twice at such sweets?

I'll put the box here, said the man, in case you change your mind. He placed it on top of a radio transmitter on the desk.

She was wearing a cap pulled down over her forehead and sunglasses, he continued, chewing a sweet, and as soon as she noticed I'd seen her—Snap! She closed her handbag. All this at a café table beside a newspaper kiosk. So I bought my paper and crossed the street. Then I made a circle round the block and reapproached the café. Do you follow me, Superintendent, I approached from the opposite direction this time?

Hector got out of his chair and walked over to the window. Go on, he said. Every day he spent more and more time looking out at the Mond Bank buildings, which grew taller and taller. Soon they would be finished, but before then, he would be gone.

I took a coffee standing at the counter, said the man, she was still sitting there and she hadn't seen me.

Hector saw a figure climbing up an invisible tower to the cabin of the highest of the two cranes. If I were him, he thought, if I were a crane driver and not a bogie . . .

Then she took off her dark glasses to read the chit so she could pay. And I recognised her! Immediately! I saw who she was. Helen. No question. Helen. Your Helen.

Why are you so sure?

Sure? Why am I so sure? Anna Helen's face has been on walls all over the city for months. With the reward printed underneath.

It's a very grainy mug shot, but it's all we had.

His visitor took another sweet and pulled at his hair.

It was her, he said, unquestionably your Helen. Have you had many people come?

Come?

To ask for the reward.

You'd be surprised.

Anyway, I didn't stop there, Superintendent, I followed her.

The man's grey hair was sparse but curly, and already sweaty. He must have pulled at it all his life. It reminded me of a newborn baby's—the same sparseness and the same dampness.

I followed her systematically. She crossed the city on foot. Already suspect, don't you think? I trailed your Helen, street by street.

So he's arrived, muttered Hector.

Who's arrived, Superintendent?

The crane driver.

I'm telling you I know where the most wanted woman in Troy lives!

Where?

Here's her address.

The man held out a slip of paper. Hector left the window and read the address.

In Gentilly . . . How do you know she lives there?

At first I couldn't believe my luck. Let me be frank with you, Superintendent, the reward is going to help us out with my pension. A million! You've got all the information you're asking for there in your hands, Superintendent.

It seems unlikely.

I saw where she went in, but I couldn't take the lift, so I didn't know which floor she was on. Do have a sweet now, Superintendent, you'll find them excellent. Then I was lucky a second time. I was hesitating, waiting in the street below, and suddenly she opened a window to shake out a carpet. The fifth floor!

Hector went back to the window. I'm listening, he said. The father crane was passing over the jib of the mother crane.

I took the lift and there I found two doors on the landing. So I rang both bells. No answer. This encouraged me, Superintendent, encouraged me because, after all, I'd seen her, she couldn't have left! If she didn't answer, it was because she was hiding!

You didn't think about the risk you were running?

Yes I did, but it was worth it. A million! We'd buy a little place in the country. And I'd already worked out my cover. I was going to be selling insurance. Car. House. Life. I think I look the part, don't you? Anyway, I rang again. Nothing. I tried to listen through the door. And then the other door opened, and there she stood in the doorway. And it was her. Your Helen.

Hector's eyes returned to the jibs. To be up there, he thought, turning in the sky above the city.

So now you know where I live, this is what she said. Could I have a few words with you, I asked, it's about insurance policies. And do you know what she replied?

Who?

The woman worth a million zloti.

Tell me.

Forget you ever saw me, Grandad! Meanwhile I was trying to manoeuvre my way to see into the flat. If you want to survive, she whispered, fuck off!

Down here on the ground, thought Hector, only the pain is true. Nothing else.

I know I've taken a great risk in coming to see you.

We'll take the matter up, said Hector. We have your address, and should we make an arrest, you'll be informed immediately. The Sergeant will show you out.

Hector turned to the window, and this time, feeling breathless, he loosened his collar. It was at this moment, after his visitor had left, that I approached him.

Do you remember your aunt who kept goats, Hector? One day in the tall grass behind her house she found a dead fox. Around the fox's sharp teeth there were traces of froth.

Hector leant his forehead against the windowpane.

Your aunt was asking herself what she should do and you appeared. Do you remember? You were fifteen.

Look what I found first thing this morning when I went out to pee! she said to you.

Leave it to me, you replied and prodded the animal with the toe of your boot.

Should I phone the mayor? your Aunt Helen asked.

No, Auntie. Forget it. You got a pick?

There's one in the hen house.

I'll bury him, you go and make us some coffee, you said.

Whilst your aunt was grinding the coffee in the kitchen, Daniel, the postman, arrived.

Do you know who's dead? he asked you.

César at Sous-Chataigne?

Yes.

A strange thing happened to me this morning, it was you who said that, Hector. I wanted to have a shit, you said, so I came over to this wall here, I slipped off my braces, and I squatted down—

God Almighty! yelled the postman. I didn't see it. Is it dead?

I felt something tickling my arse, you lied.

Not grass! said Daniel, beginning to laugh.

Imagine if I'd shat on it, you said.

You don't get rabies if you shit on a dead fox, said the postman.

I'm going to bury him double quick, you said, two metres, not a finger less.

Meanwhile your Aunt Helen was listening to the whole conversation through the window, holding her ribs and swaying on her hips with laughter. You men! she whistled, you can't even let an old woman pee on a dead fox with rabies!

For years after you left the village, she used to go on telling this story, and then she would add with pride: And today my nephew, today he's in Troy, on the police force.

There was a knock on the door.

Come in.

Report just received, sir, concerning the passports stolen from the Trans Europe Night.

When?

A week ago.

I remember, we drew a blank.

A man with one of the passports was picked up last night at the airport. Goes by the name of Pende. He's wanted on a number of narcotics charges by the heavies. Under interrogation he grassed.

On who?

He said he procured the passport from one Naisi. We had Naisi in here. You ordered his release.

There's nothing I don't remember, said Hector.

According to the description of the railway police, it seems the decoy woman may have been Naisi's sister. As for her partner, it could be a sharpie who goes by the name of Sucus. Lives in Cachan.

Do we have anything on either of them?

On the bozo, no. The bimbo's a stripper working in the Sankt Pauli.

Where's Pende now?

At the C.I.A.T.

Seeable?

Yes sir.

I'll be over, said Hector.

dear body

She was his first client. Sucus had installed himself on the corner of Third Street, a few doors down from Flores Bar. She was wearing a sleeveless dress with a taffeta bolero over her shoulders. When she sat down, she took off the little jacket and placed it on her lap. Sucus wound the elastic wrapping around her massive arm. Her flesh sagged like underdone pastry, and the way she held her head and the way she questioned with her insistent lustreless eyes proposed that all flesh everywhere was derisory. There are prostitutes whose disdain goes further than that of most nuns. As his fingers touched her, arranging the wrapping, Sucus could feel the heat of her body and it was like no heat he had ever imagined coming from a woman, for it was dry, as dry as a cricket's legs.

You've been doing this long? she asked. He nodded without daring to speak out loud. He was listening intently to hear the beat of her heart, to hear the silence come to an end. He let out the air as gently as he could, and the mercury sedately descended. She was holding her breath, suddenly anxious. All day she had had pains in her head and she feared her blood pressure was up.

Like a triumph he heard her heart coming in, and his eyes instantly flicked up to the systolic reading. He was listening to a beat that had not stopped since she was an embryo. The heart begins to beat thirty days after conception, when it is only the size of a breadcrumb. The first beat, coming from nothing, is pure gift. The first beat makes another death, before or after many passions, inevitable.

He heard the old woman's heart beating like a gong at the top of a mighty staircase in some palace. Then the gong went silent and the palace vanished. Her heart was still beating but the disk he held to her artery picked up no sound. The diastolic.

Eighteen-twelve, he said, it's a little high.

Not for me it isn't, she said, I often have twenty.

He was taking off the wrapping around her arm and she looked at him with her lustreless eyes, awaiting death, grateful for the good news, wanting a drink, wondering if he would smile.

There are medicines, he said.

Are there? She began to laugh, and her laugh turned into a cough that made her spit. You really believe there are medicines, my little love?

He helped her up from the chair and she put on her bolero.

How much do you want?

Fifteen hundred.

With the tips of the two middle fingers of her right hand she pulled the banknotes out of her bosom.

A woman of the same age but thin and with straight golden-dyed hair, wearing a trouser suit, stopped on the sidewalk beside Sucus's chair.

Harley, the woman said, I was looking for you.

Sucus pocketed the money.

Eighteen-twelve, that's what you said, isn't it?

I'll write it down for you.

No need.

That's high, Harley, said the woman in the suit.

Not for me, Fleece.

I want you to come and see Lilac.

Lilac? asked his client.

The circus number I told you about.

My memory's going, Fleece. Lilac?

Come and see for yourself.

The two women walked arm in arm down the street, stopping and turning slowly from side to side and glancing up at the sky, just as elderly ladies might do in a rose garden. Sucus immediately followed them.

Outside the Golden Fleece there were photos of girls making mouths and signs with their fingers. Sucus examined them intently. Not one of them could be Zsuzsa.

I want to rock Sucus to sleep now. I have a cradle-bed in the barn that would be almost large enough. It was made many years ago by the great-grandfather who left behind the stone sabot. I want to rock Sucus to sleep in the cradle-bed and sing him a song. A song Zsuzsa might have learnt from Rifat, the friend of her garbage man. A song that goes like this:

Sleepy night, happy day
Zero's the plaything
And nowhere nothing
That isn't in
That isn't in
Your dear body . . .

To this, all men fall asleep.

In a moment Sucus would have woken up, smiled at the girls, taken his chair back to the corner of Third Street, and found another client. But whilst Sucus was listening to my song, three brawling men woke him up, and I could do nothing. They came down the street with their arms around each other's shoulders so they shouldn't fall. They were like a single animal with reactions as slow as a bull's. They lurched into the entrance of the Golden Fleece. One of them roared: We want to see some beaver. They staggered to the box office. Another pulled out a wad of notes. Sucus watched them. When the man stuffed the change back into his hip pocket, a note fluttered like a leaf to the floor. Sucus took two strides and put his foot on the bill. It was a magenta ten thousand. He stooped, picked it up and bought a ticket.

From the beginning, men compared women with flowers, and women, enjoying it, encouraged them. They fastened blossoms in their hair, they wore perfumes, they twined leaves, and they displayed themselves. What the Bible says has never been true of the women I've known. "Consider the lilies of the field, how they grow; they toil not, neither do they spin." The women I've known only imitated flowers after they'd killed rabbits or raked hay or mucked out stables or cooked mash for the hens or carried wood from the forest. Yet still the men were right to compare us with flowers. Not because we are pure, but because, like flowers, we were created to attract. Like flowers our beauty is delicate. Like flowers the colours we were born with draw the eye to our most secret parts.

Beyond the ticket office, on the other side of the velvet curtain, the Golden Fleece smelt of beer and talc, a fermentation and a sweetness. There was no daylight and the walls were roughcast as in an underground garage. An usherette in fishnet stockings led the bull down a corridor.

Would you like number 1?

Nothing can separate us—not even a bimbo in the buff! roared one of the bull-men, we're going in together!

Sucus pushed past them to get to the end of the corridor.

What's that guy want an extra chair for?

You don't know why he's carrying his own chair?

Why should he have a chair?

Why shouldn't he?

I'll tell you why.

He'll tell us why.

To rest his cock on!

The three bull-men had well-cut suits and waistcoats. Their striped ties, loosened many times, had fallen half way down their shirts.

You'll be a bit tight, said the usherette, the berths weren't built for three.

Not even a bimbo in the buff's going to separate us!

They bundled into a cubicle the size of Yannis's crane cabin.

Ring if you want anything, said the usherette and closed the door.

Along one wall of the cubicle ran a low upholstered couch on which the three bull-men sat down, side by side. Facing them, near their knees, was a wide, inclined sheet of glass like the windscreen through which Yannis, the crane driver, looked down on the city of Troy. On the carpet by their feet was an imitation golden chalice and a neat stack of paper towels.

We're going to jerk off together, aren't we?

This is my old woman's tale. There's precious little dirt in the world I haven't cleaned up. And there's nothing—however piteous—that I haven't heard with ears that grow larger every year. With age everything else shrinks and your ears grow larger.

The light in the cubicle went off. The space beyond the windscreen remained lit but, curiously, little of this light filtered through, for the glass on the far side was opaque. The screen was made of a one-way see-through glass, first invented for prisons. Screwsglass, as it's known in the trade. Screwsglass.

We want beaver! Now!

Every light went out. The three bull-men sat in pitch darkness. Not a word was said. When the lights came up, she was there, very, very close to the windscreen. It looked as though there was scarcely space for her to stand up. She was crouching with a kimono over her shoulders, a black kimono decorated with roses. She let the garment fall slowly to the floor and then she arranged her legs differently so that she was kneeling with her shoulders and head thrown back.

The soles and heels of her feet would have revealed, to any who wanted to notice, that she had often walked barefoot.

The windscreen glass had the effect of magnifying what the men in the cubicles were staring at. This brought the woman closer to their eyes. Her pores were visible like the pock marks on the skin of an orange. Each hair of her body could be counted, each one, under the probing light, as distinct as an eyelash. She raised her hands slowly. The lights exposed traces of dirt beneath her fingernails. With her large hands she started to caress her small breasts.

Her tits are getting a hard-on! moaned part of the bull.

Small and tight! I bite! muttered another part.

Let's have the creamstick! hissed the third.

She leant forward in the lit box till her hair touched the floor. Women everywhere since the beginning of time, washing their hair, brushing, transforming to a glory, combing, platting, curling.

She twisted her hips and lay on her side, knees tucked up, a thin, thin arm between her thighs.

Show us some beaver now!

Close up against the windscreen she parted her lips with two fingers. In the village we call that part of a woman's anatomy her "nature." With two fingers she parted the ruffled lips of her nature. When a rose is still folded in its case and has never been seen, the colours of its petals can resemble what she disclosed and offered to the screwsglass.

A splintering crash reverberated through the Golden Fleece. Before the bull's six amazed and gaping eyes, a man with a folded chair smashed the lit box, felled the bimbo, broke their windscreen and struck their three heads.

Dogs were barking.

Sucus fled. In the street the prostitutes watched him run

past them. It was still daylight, the light of a late afternoon
in autumn, the moment of the year when everything in nature
is held in suspension and nothing hurries, when time slows
down, almost stops, until caught short by the night of the
first ice. Through this light Sucus was running.

As he ran, he made a wail in his head to keep out every
sound and word. The wail went up and down like the siren
of the fire engine that had come too late to put out the fire
in Cachan, up and down to the sound of Zsu-Zsa. The faster
he ran, the louder the wail.

He ran along streets thronged with people who were going
home after work and whose feet were already anticipating
leisure, liquor, soft shoes, a sofa. They stepped off the sidewalk to watch him, for his run was frantic, like that of a
hunted deer. They let him pass and immediately they looked
in the opposite direction to discover who was pursuing him
and why.

And there was nobody to be seen. Some peered across the
street, sure of finding men running along the sidewalk. There
were only bus queues, women window-shopping, several beggars. Others glanced down the side alleys, where vans were
unloading and cars hooting. Nobody was running. One man
cocked an eye up to the sky expecting a helicopter. The sky
was empty.

And Sucus ran on. He must be late for something, a matter
of life and death, the Trojans concluded, but in their heart
of hearts they knew that no man runs like that because he's
late.

The sun was going down into the dust which turned it
red.

He ran so as to never stand still again, for, should he have
stood still, he would have faced Troy and its sea and the

October sky and the galaxies and the fringe of the universe from whose unaccountable vastness no correction of the truth could ever now come.

He ran between trolley-buses and motorbikes. He ran past a Hilton hotel, a supermarket for pet food, car showrooms, travel agencies, a law court, sauna baths, bridal suites, a wool shop for babies, florists, foreign exchange kiosks, funeral parlours, coffee shops, the Trojan Horse—and not a single one of any of their promises of victory, defeat, pleasure, escape, peace, quiet, justice, soothing hands could ever be for him. So he ran faster and faster.

To the west, the lights were being switched on in the Paris Hospital, and its windows were like the portholes of a liner sailing inland. In the maternity ward, there, in the hospital on the cliff face, Yannis's wife, Sonia, had just given birth to a boy who was going to be called Alexander. Yannis was in his crane waiting for news. Sonia was exhausted, eyes ringed with sweat, blood smears on her legs the colour of the clouds in the sky, triumphant, with life before her. Give him to me, she said to the midwife who was holding Alexander upside down, give the darling to me.

His heart would soon burst, and Sucus was running to burst his heart. The blood in his throat and chest beat the time of running feet. But they were no longer his feet. She was running towards him. She was at the other end of Park Avenue and with every stride she was coming closer. Often his eyes were shut. People stepped aside for him, cleared a way, as happens for the mad. Traffic stopped and drivers smiled with a patience unimaginable for that hour in the city—as if for a few seconds they had become camel drivers in the desert. To see madness in another bestows a kind of calm. She was wearing her panther dress pulled up to the top of her thighs and she was running barefoot.

The wail did not stop, but as he ran he held out his arms towards her. He was passing Spallanzi metro station. She was running faster than ever towards him. He could see her two missing teeth and her large hands. He ran on. She was upon him and he could hear her gasping. She ran through him, clean through him.

A schoolgirl who had come up the steps from the station saw a man running towards her with his arms held out rigid in front of him. Quickly, she pressed herself against the wall. He ran past. Minutes later her pulse was still racing. She continued to tremble, not because she had narrowly escaped being run down by this man, but on account of what she had glimpsed as he passed, of his face. Its features had been so contorted that they were no longer two eyes, a nose, a mouth, ears. His face had turned into an armful of snakes and the snakes were devouring one another.

First I drive the anvil into the grass bank, then I arrange myself above it, sitting on the slope. My boots with their metal eyelets point up in the air. My woolen stockings are, as usual, a little rucked. The anvil is where it should be, between my skinny thighs, and the blade of the scythe, which I've detached from the helve, lies across my lap.

Tapping again? demands Hercule.

My eyesight's going.

Give it to me a moment. I hand him up the blade and he clicks his fingernail against it. Zing! No resonance! You can't find a good scythe these days. He flicks it again. You can hear it, can't you. No note at all. Trash!

I remember a scythe, Hercule goes on, which when you struck it, sung like a lark.

He walks slowly and painfully towards his house, where Jeanne is turning the cows out into the field, and I stay sitting on the bank, pick up my hammer, hold the blade to the anvil, and tap. I tap from the corner to the point. Drops of sweat fall on to the lenses of my glasses and the curve of the black metal blurs, blurs before my eyes.

Night fell in Troy. Sucus found himself alone by the docks, near the Customs House. There were soldiers there with a searchlight. He climbed up to the waste lot, where he had waited for Zsuzsa on their first night. There was a lamp on in the Cadillac. Sucus didn't approach. He lay on the grassy bank. Sleep, I whispered to him, sleep.

He woke to hear a voice in his ear and he turned round to see a head in the grass.

Sometimes I have good dreams, said the man who had lost both legs.

Sucus stared at him as if he, Sucus, had gone deaf and had to lip-read.

Last Tuesday, I dreamt of brandy, said the man.

The soldiers on the road below were playing with their searchlight. The man's lips were grey.

I was going to drink the whole bottle, said the man who lived in the Cadillac, and then it occurred to me it would be cleverer to leave a mouthful for the next time. So far I've not been able to get back. You look in a bad way, friend. Suppose we move over to the car, and I'll make some coffee.

Sucus said nothing.

The man with the sandals strapped to his elbows, dragged

himself up the hill. It took a long time. Sometimes he seemed to slip back like a fly climbing up a window pane. Yet compared to Sucus, he felt able-bodied and agile. This did not surprise him, for he knew that every hour in Troy invisible blows fell and destroyed limbs without a name.

In the car he found a bottle of beer and he came down the slope, loins first, like a man who still has his legs comes down a ladder.

Drink, he said, and listen to me, friend. I've thought it all out waiting for sleep in my Cadillac. With no money there's little left on the surface of this earth. It's ashes and cinders like the moon. The best thing is sleep, if you can manage sleep. In dreams money's abolished. Everywhere. Maybe you dream of money. But you never dream of paying! Nobody in the world dreams of paying. This is what makes waking up so terrible. This is what makes waking up worse than hunger. Drink your beer and get some sleep.

interrogation

The doors to the Interrogation Unit were all locked in Cauchy Street Station. To do what they do on the ninth floor they require isolation from everything else in life and death; they need to believe that there were no stories before them and that there will be none after them. God in his loneliness created the world. They up there on the ninth floor try to destroy it, member by member. So all the doors were locked.

I heard grunts, footsteps, and a voice. The voice belonged to Sergeant Pasqua although it was shriller than his everyday one. The grunts came from Sucus. The grief Sucus felt in his heart made him practically immune to the pain being inflicted on him by the sergeant. Each shock winded him, and smashed mercilessly against the inside of his skull. But between the shocks, the other pain was worse.

Who was with you? The sergeant screeched the question so many times that the four words lost their meaning. To begin with, they had referred to a gun battle on Rat Hill the previous night, during which Naisi and a police officer had been shot dead. Whowaswithyou! Whowaswithyou! With repetition the words became like a circling vulture's cry. And from far below, barely audible, came a squeak as from a mole or a field mouse. Whether its origin was the voice box or some other maltreated organ of the prisoner's body, it was impossible to tell. Then came a silence. No cry, no squeaks, no footsteps, no hum. A door opened and the silence was broken by a second voice. Hector said: I want to see the prisoner alone, Sergeant, you may go.

Sergeant Pasqua marched off. In the sound of his boots, in the rhythm of his footsteps, there was an iron pride. Then there was heavy breathing and the noise of effort, as if two men were climbing up a steep ridge.

Long ago, during one of the long summers when I was in the alpage with the goats and the two cows, Desirée and Rouquine, a strange dog appeared. A medium-sized, black dog. Nobody had ever seen him before. He was lying in the grass not far from the chalet, where there was an outcrop of grey rocks on which I sometimes used to sit to watch the valley and the clouds a thousand metres below. The afternoon was hot, the grasshoppers were hissing, and the stonechats were perching on the yellow gentian plants, which swayed whenever one alighted or flew off. The dog was clearly very old. His hind legs were so stiff that when he walked he looked as if he wanted to crap. His awkwardness was comic. Yet after watching him take a few steps, you felt a kind of pity.

Towards the end of the afternoon I saw him again. And he was unrecognisable. At first I thought he was another dog.

His hangdog tail was up and waving in furious circles. His walk was swift and brisk. He was with the brown bitch from La Fine's chalet. She must have been in heat, for both of them were sniffing and licking under each other's tails. I left them to it.

When night fell, and the stars were so bright above the pastures that they looked as if you could walk to them, he turned up again. I found him shivering in the grass when I went out to fetch some wood for the stove. He was lying in an odd position, his head was alongside his body, prodding it to see why it didn't move. With considerable difficulty I brought him inside. He stretched out beside the stove, where the pinewood was crackling, and dozed. Sleep he couldn't, for every few minutes his whole body was shaken by convulsions in his chest.

The stove quieted and the moon came up. We could see it through the windowpane that had a puddle in it. Somehow the dog got to his feet and went to the door. I opened it and he made for the rocks where I'd first seen him. There he lay down. And there he howled. Howled once. Ten minutes later he had disappeared. He had gone into the forest to die.

Men and women are not like this dog because they have words. With their words they change everything, and nothing. Whatever the circumstances, words add and take away. Either spoken words or ones heard in the head. They are always incongruous, because they never fit. This is why words cause pain and why they offer salvation.

Let's begin with your name. Tell me your full name.

You have it written down.

How do your friends call you?

I don't know.

Does the name Sucus mean anything to you?

Nothing.

Where were you yesterday around six o'clock in the evening?

I could hear the words of Sucus and the Superintendent through the locked door.

Nowhere.

Shall I remind you?

It makes no difference.

You were with a dealer named Naisi on Rat Hill and you had a Zig gun in your hands.

The sergeant told me Naisi's dead.

My man fired in self-defence.

So he's dead.

Naisi was resisting arrest and he wasn't alone, there were two other guns with him. There were three of you. All of you were firing. Naisi, his sister, and yourself.

I wasn't there.

One of my officers was killed.

He's dead.

If you weren't there, where were you?

Words were already taking Sucus and the Superintendent out of the locked room.

It was a lifetime ago.

How old are you?

You look it up.

I'm sixty-five. Your parents are alive?

My father's dead.

A Trojan?

He came from the mountains.

Like I did.

My father wasn't a bogey!

What did he do?

He was in commerce.

My father was a cattle dealer, said the Superintendent. What was your father's line?

He opened oysters.

Anything else?

He opened oysters all his life.

Do you have a regular job?

What do you expect?

So you're unemployed.

I worked on a building site.

In the city?

Across the road from here.

Where the cranes are.

Where the cranes were!

They're still there.

Are they?

Come to the window, you can see them.

There was a silence. The two men must have been standing by the window that gave on to the Mond building site.

Look! said the Superintendent, something's flying from the top of the tall crane there. It's a flag.

Flag! repeated Sucus in a broken voice.

I can't make out the insignia, said the Superintendent, my eyesight's failing.

We're on the ninth floor here, aren't we?

Can you read the flag?

White stripes and a white cross on sky-blue. Most flags don't change.

Then it's Greek, the Greek national ensign.

The crane driver was a Greek.

You knew him?

A lifetime ago. His name was Yannis. He came from the

island of Samos. He could draw a cork out of a wine bottle with his crane.

The flag wasn't there yesterday, said Hector.

Yannis flew a flag on his crane each time his wife gave him a baby, explained Sucus, he had two daughters, one of them was named Chrysanthe. He was hoping to have a son whom he would call Alexander. What more do you want to know?

I want to know where you were last night. I want to know where your guns came from. I want to know who Naisi was working for. If you tell me, I'll do my best to help you. Otherwise I must warn you, it looks bad for you. Killing a police officer isn't something we let anybody do twice.

At this point Hector probably made some sign with his hand. Perhaps a cutting-the-neck sign.

It makes no difference.

How long did you work down there?

As long as I could.

You were sacked?

I hit the foreman.

You should never hit them!

That's what Naisi said, his very words.

You admired Naisi, it seems?

Admired? Naisi tried to get by, he helped others get by. Now he's dead.

There have been very few people in my life I've admired, said the Superintendent.

You shot down Naisi.

I told you my men fired in self-defence.

It makes no difference.

I'll tell you something, young man. When I was very young, say about twelve—I hadn't left the village yet—at that age

I'd already guessed everything about life. Everything! But I didn't realise it. I thought there was a lot more to come. Of course there were things I hadn't done, things I hadn't seen, but these were details. The essentials I knew—without realising I knew them. I thought fully grown men and women—particularly women—had secrets I didn't yet know. These secrets gave them special powers, powers they could use when they were in trouble, or when they were looking for happiness. I was obsessed by these secrets. I wanted to learn them. Then I came to Troy. And after many years—for to begin with I wouldn't admit it—after many years I had to face the fact that there are no secrets. Life is like you know it when you're a kid. I don't know more than you do, but I can help you and you can help me.

There followed another silence. The two men could look at the cranes out of the window. They could look round the almost empty white-tiled room, which might have been mistaken for a dairy, except that there was no milk and there were handcuffs hanging on a wall near a gunrack. They could look at one another: Hector in his dark blue trousers and tunic, with brass crowns on his epaulettes, and his swollen hands; or Sucus, haggard, his eyes wild with loss, his jeans torn, his shirt dirtied. Whatever they looked at had nothing to do with their words. Their words were already far away, disputing the next direction they should take, insisting upon their own destination. Both men were waiting and neither knew what for.

Let's go back a few weeks to the night of October the twelfth, you were at Budapest Station.

There's never any, any, any, going back, policeman. The secret you didn't know when you were twelve was that things can be destroyed and can never be mended. Never.

You were on platform 17 in Budapest Station.

Not even God can change the past.

And you were not alone, you were with a young woman. Do you want me to tell you who she was?

Yes, say her name.

She was known as Zsuzsa.

Zsuzsa!

On the evening of October the twelfth, with this young woman known as Zsuzsa, you stole a number of passports from the schlafwagen of the Trans Europe Night.

I was alone. There was nobody else.

How did you get into the attendant's compartment?

The door was open.

Where was he?

He was talking to a lady passenger.

A lady passenger known as Zsuzsa?

I didn't know the names of the passengers, except those whose passports I grabbed.

What mountains did your father come from?

The Aravis.

How many passports did you grab from the TEN?

Fourteen.

You handed them over to Naisi?

You can't ask him!

And the name of your father's village?

The TEN passes the Aravis mountains, did you know that, policeman?

Did he want to go back, your father wanted to go back?

Yes.

Tell me the name of his village.

Its name meant lucky-horse-with-a-broken-leg.

You're lying!

He's dead. Dead, policeman, from the old German *tot-tot-tot! Tot! Tot!*

There was no reply, and it seemed that neither of the men made any effort to break the silence. For a moment I asked myself whether they had both gone, taking the inside lift like Sergeant Pasqua. Then I heard the Superintendent whisper: Can you help me? There was the noise of a chair being pulled back, followed by shuffling footsteps.

Open the window.

It doesn't open.

You have to unlock it. The key should be hanging over there by the gun rack. Can you find it? . . . That's better . . . it's good to take in some air. Your father and I, Sucus, came from the same village.

I've never seen windows with a key like this.

Prisoners try to jump.

To jump, policeman, or to kill themselves?

Tell me your papa's name.

Clement.

Clement what?

Clement Gex.

Gex!

It makes no difference now.

Your father and I were in the same class. We rode on the same luge. And, my God, he's dead. What did he die of?

TV.

I didn't quite catch . . .

I said, I'm glad he's dead.

It's not always easy between fathers and sons.

I loved him. From the early Latin *lubere*, to give something, to give pleasure.

I knew his mother, your grandmother. Angeline had the only peach tree in the village and she was very, very proud of it. The tree grew against the south wall of the house where your father lived as a boy, between the window of the kitchen and the pêle. Angeline planted it when she was young, despite your grandfather, who was against it. He said it was madness to plant peaches there. Nobody had a peach tree in the village, it would make the wall damp, and in the summer it would attract wasps. And your grandmother persisted, so that, after a number of years, it produced small juicy white peaches, about the size of billiard balls. Juicy and sharp and sweet. I can taste them on my tongue now. When there were too many wasps Angeline kept the windows shut. You're Clement's only child?

I was.

We all want to go back . . . just for a moment to look around. No, to look for something, really. Something lost. We think if we find it, we'll die happy. In my experience nobody dies happy. Perhaps somebody who's killed instantly, like Gilbert d'Ormesson on the platform. Perhaps d'Ormesson was happy when he died.

You don't look too good to me, policeman.

I think I must lie down.

Next I heard a noise that surprised and puzzled me for a moment. It was repeated like the call of the cuckoo in the spring, but its note was less liquid. A dry, squeaky sound. Suddenly it occurred to me that it was a wheel turning, and then I guessed. A trolley with rubber wheels was being pushed over the floor.

Can you lift my legs? I heard Hector say.

Both of them grunted for different reasons, Sucus with

effort and Hector with relief. Then there was a silence, a long silence from which emerged the sound of footsteps pacing up and down. Seven strides, turn, seven strides . . . The walk was repeated many times, and the steps brushed the floor softly as if they were being made in stocking feet, or by a bear in a cage.

I'm not going to make it back, declared the Superintendent in a low voice.

The steps stopped.

I've committed a murder.

What!

Last night.

Where were you?

Not on Rat Hill.

Who did you murder?

Zsuzsa.

You killed Naisi's sister!

She was my wife.

Your wife?

Naisi's sister was my wife.

So you were married, Clement's son, you were married.

Do you want to know how I killed her?

Without words there can be no repentance. With words everything can happen again, like the story I'm telling you, yet they never change what has happened.

I'm married myself, whispered the Superintendent, her name is Susanna.

But you haven't killed her. She'll be waiting for you, policeman, when you get home tonight.

Yes, she'll be waiting.

I loved her.

You killed her, you say.

You know I killed her.

I know nothing . . . It's better if I take my glasses off, said Hector.

I killed her last night.

I can see a bit better. I don't want to be taken home to the house.

I killed her last night, I tell you.

I just want to lie here.

What will they put on her?

Take off this holster, will you? It's too tight.

What clothes do they put on in the morgue?

Slip off the tunic and then it will come. Loosen the buckle.

What clothes do they put on?

Gowns.

She was so beautiful.

There's a bottle in the sink, pour me a little.

Slowly with feet that brushed the floor Sucus walked over to the sink.

Should be a glass somewhere. Take some for yourself too, said the Superintendent.

I heard the clink of a bottle and the gurgle of pouring, then Sucus's walk back across the cage.

The dead stay beautiful, said the Superintendent after a gulp, the dead don't get dirty. They stay beautiful . . . like my butterflies.

The surprise you were always expecting, said Sucus, when you were a kid, the surprise could come after death.

What was your fight about?

We didn't quarrel.

Married and you didn't fight!

I killed her without a word.

Open the window more. You're right, Clement's son, the surprise could come now, open it.

Every morning when there's snow, the robin comes to the window and I open it. I hammer the stale bread to make crumbs for him. He hops in and struts around at my feet, his little body puffed up and as round as a tangerine, his legs thinner than matches. *Mon gamin*, I tell him, *tu es le plus fidèle de tous*.

Through the locked door there was a dead silence. Then one of them said:

Do you believe in forgiveness?

It was impossible to be sure which one of them it was who asked the question. But it was the Superintendent who spoke next.

There was a curé I remember in the village, the Superintendent said, his name was Hippolyte Castor. Your father must have talked about him. He was related to your father. His sister's husband had a sister who was married to an uncle of Clement Gex. Each morning the curé Castor walked from the presbytery down to the grocer's to fetch his newspaper. I can see him now. To everybody he passed he wished a cheerful Good Day. The curé Castor was much respected, and if he was occasionally criticised for his drinking, there was always somebody to defend him, saying: Think of his life! His solitude! Wouldn't you drink from time to time. Isn't that reason enough?

Hector paused here, as if there were other reasons for drinking which he wanted to acknowledge but not name.

When the curé Castor came out of the shop, he began to read his newspaper. His feet knew their way back up the hill like a blind man's. He never for a moment looked up. Sometimes he would pause in midstride, fascinated by a news item, one leg raised off the ground like a hunting dog. Those he passed refrained, out of tact, from addressing him. He saw nothing. He walked very slowly and by the time he reached the presbytery, he knew what had happened in the world during the last twenty-four hours. This man, the curé Hippolyte Castor, said that God forgave. He said forgiveness was divine. He went further. He said if forgiving didn't exist, then God didn't exist. He said God was forgiveness.

So we are alone and unforgiven, whispered Sucus.

I'm a policeman, I'm telling you what a priest said.

How can there be forgiveness?

I'm cold. Pass me the blanket.

Suppose I catch the white ship, policeman? It was the first promise we ever made.

Leave the window as it is. The first promise?

With Zsuzsa. To take a ship.

I can see it fascinated you. It's a Beretta 921. You can take it out.

No.

The best light pistol in the world. It's not service issue, it's my own. Semi-automatic. Eight rounds . . . The pain is bad now, boy.

Where?

Everywhere. Hand it to me for a moment. Here you have what we call a second thought for the first shot. The first squeeze of the trigger is like a safety catch. It doesn't fire. You squeeze a second time and it shoots. If you want to catch the white ship, take it.

One of the men behind the door groaned.

The place is full of bogeys, policeman. I can call for help.

For God's sake, don't do that! Stay with me. Is her real name Zsuzsa?

Her real name was Lilac.

What does she do for a living?

She's dead. She worked for a gazupie.

I told you, the dead stay beautiful.

There was a thud and a gasp and I asked myself whether Sucus had hit the Superintendent. Then I heard sobbing. I had the impression both men were sobbing.

We'll go back together, we'll find the village, we'll climb up the steps to the Republican Lyre—we'll order champagne, we'll sit on the terrace. I'm too old, Hector is too old, but you're not, you're Clement Gex's son. Shout out for us both! We're back! Hector Juaradoz and Clement Gex's son are back . . . back for good, back for ever. Help! Help us!

And Lilac, policeman, can you hear me, I'm shouting so you can hear me, policeman, Lilac called me Flag!

When the shot rang out, I opened the door. It opened as innocently as any unlocked door does. The silence and still-ness in the room were equally innocent. Through the open window came the murmur of Troy's first evening traffic. The two cranes had stopped working. A tiny flag was fluttering from Yannis's masthead. Hector lay, covered with a blanket, on a surgical trolley, which was undoubtedly kept in the unit for the resuscitation of interrogated prisoners. Head thrown back, mouth and eyes wide open, he was dead. His lips were the colour of the forewings of the *Libythea geoffroji*, which is the most beautiful and rare of all the lybtheids. The same pale blueish mauve is also typical of the colour of lips after an infarctus attack. A holster, of the type that carries the gun beneath the left armpit, hung, empty, from the handle of an open cupboard beside the sink. Inside the cupboard was a pile of paper towels. Sucus, from whose heart wound blood was still seeping, was sprawled face-down on the white-tiled floor. The Beretta 921, missing from the holster, was hidden under his body. His poor finger was still around its trigger.

voyage

M oored to the dockside she dwarfs all buildings in sight. In villages, men, women, and children dream of palaces. The poorer the home, the more perfect the palace. And the white ship is a floating palace. All her cabins are first-class and each one is different, with its own furniture and fittings and mementos. Voyagers who were homeless or exiled, passengers who lived all their lives in institutions are given, on my ship, the room of their dreams.

A small detail distinguished her from other liners when she was moored in the Trojan docks: on her seven decks there was not a single lifeboat or lifebelt to be seen. The few passersby who noticed this strange fact argued amongst themselves about what it might mean. Some maintained that lifeboats were automatically ejected from below-deck in case of

an emergency. Others shrugged their shoulders and simply
asserted that on such a ship, with such a reputation, they
were not needed!

Naisi's cabin was a conservatory such as might belong to
an emperor, filled with flowering plants, among the greenery
of which stood a piano and a synthesizer. On the floor were
carpets from Aleppo whose woven flowers were as geometric
and beautiful as the scrolls on banknotes. The colours of
their weaving were beyond price. Beiges of honey, and blues
of wood smoke in the evening light. Naisi, dressed in a pair
of swimming shorts and seated in a wicker chair like a sun
god was experimenting with a rendering of "Your Balls Are
Hanging Out" on the synthesizer. The wounds in his chest
were healed. Their scars had turned into tattoos, just as,
over the centuries, gardens turn into flourishes on rugs. The
largest tattoo, made from the wound that killed him, showed
the palm of an open hand.

On another deck, in another cabin, Officer Frey, the policeman Naisi shot dead the day before during the siege of
the Blue House, was preparing brochettes of fish. He was
dressed in a loose anorak, like an Eskimo, with a hood over
his head. The walls of his cabin were made of logs and had
bearskins nailed to them. The grill of an electric oven was
already alight, ready to cook the fish he was preparing. By
his bedside lay a husky. Over the cabin radio came an Arctic
weather report announcing temperatures of minus forty cen-
tigrade. He too was happy.

Sucus and the Superintendent were among the last to
embark, and I received them as they came up the gangway
together.

Welcome Superintendent, I said to Hector. How well you
look! On C Deck you'll find a bar called the Café de la Paix.

A young woman who serves drinks there has already prepared a glass for you.

To Sucus I said: In cabin 316, the one next to yours, there is someone waiting to see you, little redstart.

. . .

Come in, said Naisi, when Sucus knocked on his cabin door.

It's you! I thought you'd be gone already! said Sucus.

Make yourself at home.

What a cabin you've got!

The white roses knocked me over, said Naisi.

They're snow queens.

Sucus went over to the porthole. I can see the Hotel Patrai, he said.

I can't, said Naisi, nowhere.

Beyond the storage tanks there.

Nowhere.

Not those, the Exxon ones.

Show me your wound, said Naisi.

Sucus took off his shirt. By his heart there was a scar, with stitches still in it, in the form of a Z.

I never thought you'd be on this ship, Sucus said again.

She leaves every third day.

I thought every night.

Once, long ago, she used to. The schedule changed in Jerusalem at the time forgiveness began.

You talk about forgiveness like a bogey, Naisi.

Everyone on this ship is happy. So many passengers, and not a single tragedy, no grief!

Hundreds of passengers?

Thousands.

I heard what happened from Pasqua, said Sucus.

This ship'll never take him! said Naisi.

You think he's immortal?

They'll throw Pasqua in the water for the crabs. He'll be taken nowhere.

And the bogey's forgiveness?

You're forgetting something, Brother-in-Law. There are certain things which are unforgivable.

Do you know what I did? asked Sucus.

You used a Beretta 921. A black villain, isn't she? I adore the Berettas. With her little black tail like a pig!

Who told you?

The herons. *Tzaplia* in Russian. Creatures from far away who bring a message.

So they know everything, the herons.

Not everything. Only the Devil knows all. Which is why ignorance is good. Stay ignorant, Brother-in-Law.

Where do you see the herons?

They come when the music plays.

It's bound to come back, the grief, said Sucus.

. . .

Where are you going? asked Naisi later.

To the village, my father's village.

Funny how our fathers come back, isn't it? I've been thinking about it. Once they could save us from everything, our fathers, and so we go on believing it. I guess that's why I'm going to Aleppo.

Do you know what I did, Naisi?

With the little black villain, yes.

It's bound to come back, the grief.

Let's get a drink, said Naisi. There's a bar on the deck above with a little dancing lawn out back.

The two men walked slowly up a wide staircase, between two mosaics the colour of a lake depicting many sorts of birds, and in the foreground of each one herons.

Tzaplia, said Naisi nodding at them.

Do you know what I did, Naisi?

Yes, I told you.

Naisi . . .

I'm listening.

Have you seen Zsuzsa on board?

Zsuzsa!

She has to be here.

You're out of your mind, Brother-in-Law.

I killed her.

You could never have done that. Never.

Sucus killed Zsuzsa, whispered Sucus.

There are words said which have no expression. Their flatness says all. Before these three words Naisi opened his arms, and Sucus flung himself between them. For several weeks they stayed like that, embraced at the top of the stairway.

. . .

Installed at a corner table in the Café de la Paix, Hector was singing. As he sang, he looked softly but fixedly ahead, as if peering at a rock a few feet from his face. In this rock he heard other voices singing the same songs from his childhood.

A barmaid brought him a double mommi. Placing the ice-cold glass on the table, she poured in the water, for she knew exactly how strong Hector liked his drink, and the liquid turned milky, like a pearl. Then she sat down and quietly sang with him. Days passed before he noticed her, but when at last he did, his face broke into such a broad smile that he had to stop singing.

You know all the words? he enquired.

I learnt them for you.

Let me get you a drink.

I don't need one.

My wife always needed a drink, said the Superintendent. When she drank her first glass at eleven in the morning, she raised her thin child's arm way above her head and her little feet in buckled shoes had to trot fast to keep up with the adult legs crossing the lawn by the dovecoat, whose beady birds frightened her, and when the first gulp of liquor lifted the first weight off her head, her father's large hand, more protective than Achilles' shield, grasped hers, at eleven every morning, and they walked together, the dead father and the frightened daughter, across the gravel path to confront . . . whatever the day might bring. I know all that now.

I want you to be happy, said the woman opposite him.

Then let's sing again.

They sang: *Delà la mer, il y a t'un pré*.

It's beyond me, said the Superintendent, how you remember every song.

All of us purser's staff, all of us on this ship, explained the barmaid, are volunteers.

You know every song I know.

We had not given enough pleasure during our lives. So to make up for it, we volunteered as crew on this ship's world cruise. A world cruise takes one minute.

Let's sing "Sweetheart, Your Eyebrows Are Pencil Thin,"
said Hector.

. . .

The ship had long since weighed anchor. On the open deck
it was dark, or dark again. The waves of the black water
were slow and wide, like those of an ocean.

A tanker passed by to port, but the officer on her bridge
saw nothing and her radar screen recorded nothing, because,
to other vessels at sea, the white ship was now indistinguish-
able from the night.

We have to find her, Naisi finally said at the top of the
staircase, she must be on board.

I'll take A Deck, said Sucus, and you take B, as soon as
one of us finds her . . . we tell the other.

Below deck everything was lit like a mountain slope of
snow at noon when there's not a cloud in the sky. Every grain
of my ship sparkled that night.

Both men had but a single purpose: to find Zsuzsa. Yet
neither hurried, for time could not rob them.

Sucus heard faint music coming from the ballroom at the
stern end of A Deck, and he decided to look there first, in
case she was dancing. He strolled down an aisle of shops—
which was like a street in a city, except that there were no
poor—towards the music. Suddenly he stopped before a window to look at a jersey dress, tight-fitting, with black spots
like a panther.

At the same moment, he felt a pressure against the back
of his knees and against his shoulder blades. He wanted to
extend his hand and touch her hip as he usually did, but he
did not dare.

He simply stood there without moving, for a year, and

towards the end of that time he learnt that only a body can forgive a body, and that forgiveness, if it comes, comes from a honeycomb of tenderness secreted by the bodies concerned. His eyes shut before the shop window, he saw how forgiveness could never be the consequence of judgement. Forgiveness was not a principle, but a brush of lips on closed eyes. The prefix *for* in *forgiefan*, Old English, meant, like the Greek *peri*, enclosing, encircling, embracing.

He turned round to face Zsuzsa. No one was there, yet the word *forgiefan* persisted in his head and became part of the music that was still playing, and towards which he now walked. In the ballroom Sucus danced alone through the throng of dancing passengers. He was now sure to find her. Forgiefan.

On B Deck Naisi passed a casino. He could feel the quiet of held breath through the curtain, and this he could not resist. He slipped in. Zsuzsa was not there. The croupier wore a silver suit with wings on its back. When Naisi approached, the wheel was turning slowly, the ball jumping like a finger that teases over the spine's vertebrae. It stopped on seventeen. The players who had lost turned away.

Tell me what you wish, sir, said the croupier smiling at Naisi, are you playing to lose?

Nope.

To win then. You wish to win.

No, to gamble.

You want to gamble, really?

Yes, to risk all.

Passengers have little to risk, sir.

I'll find something.

If you want to buy chips, sir, the bank's over there.

The cashier was a boy of ten wearing white gloves.

Listen, Naisi said to him, I've seen you before. You lived on Rat Hill, didn't you? Your name's Kaddour, you died of typhoid fifteen years ago.

The boy nodded, smiling.

Listen, Kaddour, I need to shoot for the sky.

Then tell me what you're buying with.

I've got a piano in my cabin.

The boy shook his head, although he still smiled.

If I win, said Naisi, supposing I win, I need to collect a bundle, a figure with countless noughts, Kaddour.

If you want to win, said the boy, I'll give you five chips, if you want to lose I'll give you fifty. You don't have to buy them.

No, said Naisi, I need to wager. Can't you understand that? If I win, I want to say to my sister—you remember Zsuzsa, Zsuzsa's somewhere on this ship—when I find her, if I've won, I want to say to her: Here. They're yours. Take it. Get everything you want . . . everything!

Then what are you buying with, Naisi?

Naisi hesitated. His pockets were empty. He could hear the wheel turning behind him, and he imagined how he would go up to Zsuzsa, who at this moment was probably dancing in the ballroom, and how he would tap her on the shoulder . . . All right, he said at last, I've an idea. Can I bet my place in this story? Can I buy with that?

The boy stared at him, his eyes wide open with admiration.

If I lose, said Naisi, I'm erased!

The boy handed him a hundred chips.

Meanwhile the years passed. Naisi won. Hector dreamt of butterflies by night and sang songs during the day. I mostly sat aft on the top deck, looking back towards the ship's wake. I love the way the white turbulence of the water turns to calm astern, and I love the surf as it disperses and recedes and becomes like pieces of lace clinging to the ocean's skin.

. . .

Sucus and Naisi met at the top of the heron staircase.

No? asked Naisi.

No.

Then she must be on C Deck.

You go forward and I'll take the stern.

I've just won a bundle for her, said Naisi, now she can have everything. Everything.

I told her, said Sucus, I told her when we did the passports, that I wanted to take her to the village and now we're going there, we're going to Lucky-Horse-with-a-Broken-Leg.

The two men were dreaming of Zsuzsa's pleasure.

Aft on C Deck there was a hairdresser's. He looked carefully under each dryer to make sure the woman sitting there wasn't Zsuzsa. Next to the hairdresser's was a cinema. How was he going to tell in the dark whether she was there? He went and stood in front of the screen and cried: Lilac, I love you! Then he waited. If she was there, she would reply. The audience was quieter than ever. Lilac, I love you! Silence. He turned round to look for the first time at the picture on the screen. He saw Zsuzsa. Zsuzsa was washing his hair outside the Blue House.

Out on deck the wind was plucking at the rigging and the white paintwork was dazzled. The ship had reduced speed and the water had changed its character. It was no longer ocean but inland sea, without swell and almost without waves. Its calm corresponded to Sucus's conviction of being forgiven. Leaning over the ship's railing, he saw a sheep's head, apparently floating in the water below. The sheep was alive. Its head turned. He saw another, then another. The ship was passing a whole flock of sheep. They couldn't be swimming, he told himself, their feet must be on the ground.

. . .

Amidships the two men met.

So she's in her cabin, said Naisi.

I think she's forgiven me, Sucus said.

I told you . . .

You said there were things which are unforgivable.

I said that too. Let's try the cabins.

They'll be locked.

No problem. The purser calls them cabins, but you know what they really are.

Yes, said Sucus, our tombs.

So we just read what's written on them. We'll find her in no time. In no time. Have you been in your cabin yet?

I've been too busy searching.

You'll be surprised when you go in.

Tell me.

It's a stable full of cows!

Shit! said Sucus.

You must have chosen it.

They looked at each other, surprised by what the heart claims and the mind doesn't know.

The ship had reached the Aravis mountains. It was early morning and the grass it was sailing over was still white with frost. The cuckoo was already repeating his call. The ship's engines were making less noise than a tractor. Redstarts, chaffinches, coal-tits, swallows flew, chirping, warning, singing, between the orchards and greniers. I could hear them from my chair on deck. Everybody and every creature that morning had a hundred years to live. As the sun rose, the grass lost its frost and became green.

The black branches of the fruit trees, at the level of the lowest portholes, had just opened into white flowers, but their leaves were still folded. On the starboard side of the valley, behind a chapel, a giant apple tree in blossom looked like a cloud, the size of a pocket handkerchief. Only the rock face above the village was still half veiled in mist. As the sun rose higher, the fields on every side changed colour. From green to radiant yellow. They changed, as millions of dandelions opened their petals together.

I'll do F Deck, you do E, said Sucus, and, walking slowly down corridors of cabins at the level of the fruit trees, he read inscription after inscription. None mentioned Zsuzsa. Naisi came running down a companionway from the deck above and grasped Sucus's arm.

No?

No.

Naisi, listen, supposing—supposing she's not on this ship!

Then she's alive.

Yes?

Yes.

She's alive!

I read it from the start, from the first evening I arrived, mused Naisi. Nobody can dream of how many different kinds of happiness there are on a ship like this.

The ship cast her anchor. And one by one the cows in Sucus's cabin came down the gangway to the meadow. They placed their feet with great deliberation and care, like city women in high-heeled shoes do when walking over cobblestones. Once they reached the grass, they kicked up with their hind legs, they jumped, they charged each other with their horns, and they ran in circles. Delphine, who had had six calves, leapt as high as a goat.

I was sitting under my pear tree when the white ship sailed away to become the mountain that is always covered in snow. The cows waded deep into the grass of my orchard where they tasted, smelt, licked, swallowed, and ate so much that when they lay down under the trees to chew, they dozed. Sucus was stretched out in the grass not far from where I was sitting.

You see on the *adret*, he told me, you see the field up there, you see its yellow? That's the yellow of Zsuzsa's earrings, the ones which were big enough to pass a lemon through.

Then he wept for a millenium, there in my grass beside me.

When all was done and his eyes were dry, he stared at the sky and said: If I become that blue, old woman, nothing, nothing any more will separate me from Zsuzsa.

Yes, I whispered, I have taken off your coat of bees, yes, no more words . . . Sleep, Sucus, sleep. She's alive.

I t is possible you have been to Troy without recognising the city. The road from the airport is like many others in the world. It has a superhighway and is often blocked. You leave the airport buildings which are like space vessels never finished, you pass the packed carparks, the international hotels, a mile or two of barbed wire, broken fields, the last stray cattle, billboards that advertise cars and Coca-Cola, storage tanks, a cement plant, the first shanty town, several giant depots for big stores, ring-road flyovers, working-class flats, a part of an ancient city wall, the old boroughs with trees, crammed shopping streets, new golden office-blocks, a number of ancient domes and spires, and finally you arrive at the acropolis of wealth.

Should you visit Troy again, you will recognise Zsuzsa. It is impossible that you won't now be able to pick her out from among the many thousands of faces, that fill the streets and corners and stations of the city every night. You would recognise her even from far away. Perhaps she will be singing for money in a train on the Eddington Line. Perhaps she will be seated, waiting, on a high stool against a bar, skirt pulled high up and legs crossed, in Sankt Pauli. Perhaps she will be married, the mother of several children, and when you pass her she will be pushing a pram. I do not know, for her life is not yet over.

Perhaps you will recognise her in one of the aisles of Santa Barbara where she will have gone to pray. Wislawa will go, whenever she can, to the same cathedral to pray for Branch and Sucus. Despite her losses, her poor health, her eyes, her poverty, Wislawa will find the strength to continue a little longer, for she has perched in the tree of God. I do not know whether the two women will ever meet there, where the mosaics on the floor tell the story of Saint George.

Perhaps it will be in the Champ-de-Mars that you will pick out Zsuzsa and she will be on her way to visit somebody in prison. If you dare go to Rat Hill, perhaps she will be living there in another shack, and she will look like an old woman.

Poverty, loss, pain, passion, time, or money will have marked her eyes, her hands, her mouth, and the way she holds her arms and the way she places her feet, but they will not, I think, have changed her soul; in order to play this world she will still believe, and make others believe, that she's its centre, its prize, and its capital, and she is probably right.

If you doubt and ask yourself whether it's really her, and

you're lucky enough to be close to her, you'll be able to know by her two missing teeth and the long scars on her scalp, only partly hidden by her unruly, once-black hair . . . that it is really Zsuzsa.

Don't fret, my little one. Fly! Everything's going to be all right. Fly, my Heart.